Lovely Oblivion: Polly

A.D. Craig

Copyright © 2021 A.D. Craig
All rights reserved. No part of this book may be reproduced or used in any manner without the prior written permission of the copyright owner. With the exception of public figures, any resemblance to persons living or dead is coincidental. The opinions expressed are those of the characters and should not be confused with the author's.

Chapter 1
Flynn

"Thanks for spending the night with me," Flynn said.

He stood from his makeshift bed of blankets on the floor. He ran his hands over his hair, then looked down at his slept-in clothes. *Ah fuck.* He tried to smooth out some wrinkles, to no avail.

Polly stood and stretched sleepily from the hotel bed. Her long blond hair fell in a ruffled mess. But her jeans and t-shirt looked no worse for the wear after she'd slept in them.

"Anytime. You pick the best movies," she said.

Polly smiled at him then crossed the room to the hotel room's kitchenette. She poured a packet of ground coffee into the room's standard coffeemaker, started it, and disappeared into the bathroom. The door shut firmly behind her.

Flynn picked the covers up off the floor and tossed them on the bed. He pressed his glasses onto his nose — he only needed them for reading, but they were necessary or words fuzzed together. Then he found the room service menu on the nightstand by the phone and called its number to order them breakfast.

After he ordered, he sat at the room's small table, shoved the empty pizza boxes from last night out of the way, and flipped through the local attractions pamphlet. Not that he'd have time to visit anything in that town; he was leaving in an hour.

Polly opened the bathroom door and stepped out. She had combed her hair and washed her face. Even without makeup, the woman looked beautiful. Flynn removed his glasses and tossed them on the table.

"We need to get breakfast," she said.

"Ordered. Room service is on the way."

She grinned and danced in place. "Awesome."

She plopped onto the bed and turned on the TV. A random movie played. She cupped her hands behind her head and eyed the movie.

"Where's your next stop on the tour?" he asked.

"Houston. Then Birmingham and up the east coast."

Polly played bass and sometimes guitar in a successful punk rock band. Her heart always returned to her guitar. Her band, Lovely Oblivion, was currently mid-tour around the U.S.

Flynn played guitar for another popular band, Late Nyght Smoke.

Polly and Flynn's paths crossed sometimes in the music industry, but they rarely found themselves in the same place. The friends only saw each other a few times a year, but made a point to get together for adventures whenever they did.

"We're touring up the west coast then flying east later this summer," he said. "Will you be in Boston?"

"We will. When are you going to be there?"

"August 24."

Polly nodded. "Me too. See you then?"

"Absolutely." Flynn smiled. "Wanna do another sleepover?"

"Of course. I wouldn't miss it."

A knock sounded at the door. Flynn stood and answered it.

The teen from room service stammered when he saw Flynn. "Mr. — Flynn — Breakfast." He gestured at the cart.

Flynn grinned and slipped the teen a $100 tip. "Thanks, man."

Flynn wheeled the cart into their room and shut the door in the star-struck teen's face.

He steered the cart to the table and slid their meals into place. He also set out two mini bottles of syrup.

Polly flopped out of bed and walked to the coffee pot to get their coffee ready. She poured the coffee into disposable cups, adding a ton of cream and sugar to hers but leaving his black. She carried the cups to the table and set them down by their plates.

She pulled the cover off her plate as she sat down. Eggs, bacon, and pancakes. Flynn grinned when her eyes lit up.

Flynn sat in his chair and removed the cover from his own plate, his tattooed arms flexing as he did. He inhaled the scent of eggs and bacon. Amazing.

Polly picked up one of the syrup bottles and opened it. She spread the maple liquid all over her food. Then she lifted her fork and dug into the eggs. She chewed, then moaned as the flavor hit her tongue.

Flynn smiled. His fans considered him a badass asshole with no heart. His public image. But he definitely had a heart, and it had a soft spot for this woman. He considered her one of his dearest friends, even if they didn't see each other in person often enough, and he would do anything for her. Only Polly got to see his soft side.

"Thanks for ordering breakfast. This is great," she said.

"You betcha." He sipped his coffee.

"I want to visit Boston with you when we get there," she said.

"Where do you want to go?"

"I don't know. Nowhere in particular. Can you work on an itinerary for us?"

"Me?" he asked, surprised. "I don't know how good I'd be at that. I don't do much of the planning."

"Me either. You make an itinerary and I'll make one, then we'll merge them when we get to Boston. Hit all the best highlights. It doesn't have to be perfect."

"How long will you be there?"

"Two days."

"Okay, I'll give it a shot."

"That's all I ask. Thank you."

Flynn nodded. "Don't forget to take some cool pictures and send them to me before Boston. I want to see the east coast through your camera." Besides kicking ass on guitar, Polly took photos for fun — and Flynn loved them. He often told her she should photograph professionally.

Polly laughed. "Yes, sir."

Flynn hissed. "Eww. No. Don't call me sir. If you insist on using a title, 'Master' is acceptable." He wiggled his eyebrows at her.

She laughed for almost a minute, holding her stomach because she laughed so hard.

Flynn chuckled.

She said with a formal British accent, "Thank you for the laugh, Master Flynn. I most enjoyed it."

Flynn groaned and pressed a hand over his eyes. "Oh, God. I've created a monster."

"Oh dear, Master Flynn. Is there something the matter?"

Polly continued the rest of breakfast with a fake accent.

They finished the food and sat at the table for a while, talking back and forth in fake accents. Soon, Polly's phone chimed on the nightstand.

She crossed the room to grab it. She silently viewed the text on the screen.

She said, "It's a 'get back to the bus' text from my tour manager, Greg. I should probably head out."

"Yeah, I need to head to my people, too. I expect the 'where are you' texts to start anytime now."

Polly grinned and pretend-curtsied. She continued with the fake accent. "Many thanks, Master Flynn. I much appreciated the pizza, beer, and movie night. I shall see thee in Boston."

"Yes, you shall."

Flynn stood from his chair and crossed the room to wrap her in a hug. She reminded him of their height difference when her hair tickled his chin. She hugged him back.

He said, "It was good to see you. Don't forget to send me pictures."

"I will." She stood back and looked at him. "Try to stay out of trouble."

He smirked. "I'll try but no promises."

Polly rolled her eyes, but then she smiled. "Take care. I'll see you in a couple months."

"You too. I'll see you soon. Text me."

Flynn walked her to the door and waved her off as she walked down the hall to the elevator. He closed the door behind him and heard the first text chime on his phone as he plopped on the bed.

Chapter 2
Polly

"What did that idiot do now?" Polly asked rhetorically as she watched the cops slap cuffs on Flynn on the bar's TV. The cops shoved his muscular physique into a cruiser.

She pressed her hand over her eyes and shook her head as the blue lights flashed and the cop car pulled away on screen.

"Again? They're mid-tour. He'll probably miss some shows. Man, I'm glad he's not on our tour," Jade said. She drank a sip of lemonade. Jade had tied her rainbow hair up in a bun and tucked it under a ball cap to lower recognition. Polly wore a ball cap too, her blond hair pulled into a ponytail that stuck from the back of her hat.

Polly and Jade, two members of the popular punk rock band Lovely Oblivion, had dodged the paparazzi to go to an inconspicuous sports bar for dinner in the random town they were staying in for the tour. So far, so good — no one recognized them.

"I can't believe he got arrested again," Polly said. She sighed and removed her hand from her eyes. She picked up her fork and continued to eat her dinner, which was tasty glazed chicken and a baked potato.

"At least he's not our problem," Jade said. "I worry enough about our crew and the people on our buses. Someone like him would give me a heart attack."

"He's not really a bad person, but he makes impulsive choices. They aren't always great," Polly said.

Flynn and Polly spent time together as friends when their paths crossed and texted each other regularly. They were close enough friends that his arrest worried her...again.

Someone changed the channel. The new newscast showed the arrest from another angle. Flynn's face flashed the camera, his crew cut hair, green eyes, and cheeky grin hit the camera as the cops loaded him into the cruiser.

Polly shook her head and breathed a sigh of relief. Okay, Flynn wasn't worried. She would try not to, either. Still, she hoped nothing bad happened to him.

"We have fifteen more live performances then studio time. It'll be nice to have a break and stay in one place for a few months," Jade said, breaking Polly's train of thought.

"Where are you and Mr. Blue Eyes staying?" Polly asked. Jade didn't have a residence, preferring to couch surf because of the musician's lifestyle. Her fiancé Ryker, a former Navy SEAL who the band liked to call Mr. Blue Eyes, had a home in the mountains but it was very rural and hours away.

"While we're recording, Ry and I will rent monthly or sublet somewhere near the studio. Once the album's done, we'll go to his cabin for a while."

"Mmmm. Okay, so when's the wedding?"

Jade laughed. "We haven't decided yet. Soon. Probably not until next year. I'm trying to convince Ryker to do Vegas but he doesn't want to."

"Why not?"

"He thinks I would miss the ceremony too much and regret it later. But I wouldn't. I only want to be married to the guy." She shook her head and sipped her lemonade.

"We'll help you plan something soon if you want."

"Tomorrow, courthouse?"

Polly laughed. "You know what I mean. Something that makes you both happy."

"The man needs to hurry up and marry me so we can have a billion kids."

Polly held her hands up in a stop gesture. "Whoa, whoa, whoa. We have to talk about this. I know Bex had a baby in the musician's life, but she's our lead singer. You're the drummer. I doubt you can drum while you're pregnant."

"I can! I looked it up. Drumming is considered an exercise. The danger is that it raises heart rate. As long as I was drumming before pregnancy and I'm used to doing it, I'm good. The vibrations won't hurt a baby."

Polly looked at her, an eyebrow raised. "You researched this?"

"Yes. I mean, Ryker and I aren't planning anything right now, but I wanted to know. Drumming is my life. And I adore Chloe." Chloe was their lead singer Bex's one-year-old girl. The band was collectively raising Chloe on tour. They all spoiled that baby.

Polly shook her head. "Enjoy life for now. We'll only be touring for maybe ten years. After that, the musician's lifestyle is over. Take it day by day, enjoy the unique lifestyle, and don't rush commitment," she said.

Jade laughed. "I'm sure Grady appreciates that outlook."

Polly's fiancée, Grady, still lived in their hometown. He wanted roots, but he understood Polly's need for music and travel. He stayed in their hometown, saying he would work on a home for them so they'd have somewhere to go when she was ready to settle. Grady worked a comfortable 9-5 as an accountant. He didn't have to work because of Polly's income, but he chose to. Polly's life was wild compared to Grady's. The two were the definition of "opposites attract."

"He gets it," Polly said. "We've talked about it."

They'd been dating since high school. Grady was nothing but patient. He'd popped the question, but he wanted to wait for Polly to settle down to get married and move in together.

"We need to get everyone engaged. Lyra and Maggie still need rings. Then we can do a mass onstage band wedding," Jade said. "All of us can attend and we can broadcast it for publicity. I mean, I know Bex is already married but she can renew."

Polly laughed. "That will not meet your 'marry Ryker as soon as possible' deadline."

"True. Nevermind. I was thinking out loud. Badly." Jade shook her head.

Polly flagged down their server and requested the check.

Once they paid, they would head back to the bus and travel to the next city.

* * *

Polly stretched out inside her bunk on the bus, in the dark with the curtain closed, the wheels whirring rhythmically underneath. The only light came from the glow on her phone.

She texted Grady the photos she'd taken at the beach of the waves, the band, and Chloe. She thought they looked phenomenal. The messages showed "read," but no response came. She checked the time. 1:30 am. She shrugged it off. Grady was probably sleeping and would reply in the morning.

She texted a picture of the waves to Flynn.

He immediately replied, *"Gorgeous. Which beach?"*

They texted back and forth about their travels and where they'd been. Polly eventually sent more pictures of the band.

Flynn: Fantastic
Polly: Thank you
Flynn: Wch magazine?
Polly: What?
Flynn: Wch magazine shld I buy these in?
Polly: None right now. These aren't magazine quality.
Flynn: Disagree
Polly: Maybe next time
Flynn: Realy think u should
Polly: Maybe someday
Flynn: U should
Polly: Tell me about the arrest I saw on TV
Flynn: Shit, u saw that?
Polly: I did. Grin and all
Flynn: I regret nthing
Polly: I could tell
Flynn: Drunk dude abusd server at bar. I mde him stop
Polly: Not the whole story
Flynn: With my fist

Polly: More accurate.
Flynn: Tablds r having a field day. Thy make me snd awful. Dn't read that trash. Unblvble how they mix trth and lies
Polly: That's normal. What happened at court?
Flynn: Judge gve warning. Sd guy was lcky I got to him 1st
She laughed.
Polly: He did not
Flynn: Mbe, mbe not — that's how I rember it
Polly: I think your memory may be faulty
Flynn: Nope, nvr accused of that b4
Polly: What if I accuse you now?
Flynn: Deny, deny, deny
Polly: Are you okay at least?
Flynn: Yes. Thank u
Polly: Where are you tonight?
Flynn: San Fran
Polly: I'm between Birmingham and the next stop
Flynn: Nice. Did show. Hotel 2nite, show trw, then bus north
Polly: How's the Boston itinerary?
Flynn: Great. Hope you're rdy
Polly: Looking forward to it
Flynn: Looking fwd to more pics. Rest up. C u soon. Night
Polly: Night

* * *

Grady texted back the next day. She got the response at lunchtime when she woke up and messaged him back.

Grady: Nice pics
Polly: Thank you
Grady: You should make a scrapbook from your tour and include them
Polly: I don't know how to scrapbook but maybe I can try
Grady: Sure, give it a shot

  Polly: *Fifteen more performances then I'll be in one place for studio time. Maybe you can come visit? I can come home after we record but I'll be at the studio at least through September*
  Grady: *Let me know the dates and I'll try to get some time off work*
  Polly: *Okay, I will.*
  Grady: *I've got to get back to the office. Lunch is over. Love you*
  Polly: *I love you too. Have a nice day*

  She laughed when she opened her unread texts to find a selfie of Flynn looking at the camera with a grin while holding a half full bottle of whiskey by his face. He appeared to be at a hotel afterparty.

  Someone would be hungover today.

  Polly shook her head and turned on some music from her playlist. She laid her phone on the bunk beside her.

  She no longer heard the road under the tires, so they must be parked somewhere. Probably outside that night's venue.

  She laid in her dark bunk, enjoying the soft music from her phone, staring at the bunk's fabric-lined ceiling, and taking a moment of peace. Between paparazzi, the schedule, and being on the road, musician life could be chaotic — but Polly loved it and wouldn't change a thing.

TABLOID NEWS
"BRAWL"

America's favorite troublemaker, Flynn Morgan, caused yet another bar fight this week. You may remember him as the handsome, heartless guitarist from Late Nyght Smoke who caused an uproar a few years ago when he senselessly ended his relationship with America's Sweetheart, top model Anika Evans. We love to hate him! Dubbed "heartless" after their breakup, Flynn again showed and proved his heartless state when he started tonight's bar fight with an innocent bystander without reason. Reports say a female server sparked the fight. More on this story later.

Chapter 3
Polly

"Tuesday's show is cancelled. The venue had a water line burst and it flooded their vendor area. The damage won't be repaired before the show, and they can't have patrons around the damage," their tour manager Greg announced to the band, who sat in the front lounge of the bus. "Today's Sunday. You've got a show on Saturday. If you promise me you'll show up by 11 am Saturday morning at the venue in Richmond, you can have an unscheduled vacation until then."

Cheers went up around the room and no one asked any questions. Everyone scrambled to their bunks to pack their bags.

Perfect, Polly thought. She could surprise Grady. The opportunity to enjoy some time together for a few days happened so rarely, she was sure he'd be thrilled to see her.

Polly packed her duffel bag and set it on her bed, then pulled out her cell phone. She brought up the browser and navigated to the airport to buy a plane ticket. She could get a ticket today to an airport about an hour from home. If she got a rental car and drove, she could be in her hometown by nightfall.

Quickly, Polly booked her airline ticket and reserved a rental car. She and their keyboardist, Maggie, caught a car to the airport together. Maggie had pulled her long black hair into a ponytail and donned a hat. Polly tied her blond hair up in a scarf and removed all her makeup. With any luck, no one would look twice at them.

"I can't wait to see Grady. I haven't seen him since the last break and that seems like forever ago," Polly said.

"That's great. I hope you two have a blast. My friend's having an art show in Brooklyn. I'm so excited I get to go."

Polly grinned. "That's awesome. I can't believe the schedule worked out so well."

Maggie laughed. "I told my friend it must be fate."

The car pulled up to the curb at the drop-off for the airport. They unloaded their bags and headed inside.

"Have a safe trip," she told Maggie and hugged her.

"Take care, I'll see you soon," Maggie said.

They separated and went to the waiting areas for their respective planes. Luckily for Polly, no one recognized her.

* * *

Polly pulled the silver rental car into the driveway in front of their house — the one Grady had carried her into two years ago, proposed to her in the bedroom, and told her was theirs. No other cars were in the driveway. Night had fallen, so it was obvious no lights were on in the two story brick house at the end of the cul-de-sac. Huh. Weird. Maybe Grady had to work late.

Polly parked and pulled out her phone to text him.

Polly: Where are you?

His reply arrived quickly.

Grady: Bed

Polly pocketed her phone, climbed out of the car, and went to the front door.

She tried her key in the door, but it didn't work. How odd.

She put her keys away and knocked loudly.

Silence.

She knocked again.

The wind whipped past and rustled her hair. Probably blowing in a storm. Down the road, she heard a dog bark. Still, silence from the house. She tried to peer into the window by the door, but it was too dark for her to see anything.

She pulled out her phone and texted Grady again.

Polly: At home?

Grady: No, I'm on a work trip. Will be home tomorrow

Polly: Okay, sweet dreams

Grady: Sweet dreams

She walked back to the car and climbed in. Grady hadn't said anything about a work trip but maybe he'd forgotten to tell her.

She buckled her seatbelt, turned on the car, and backed out of her parking spot.

Polly drove the twenty-five minutes across town to her parents' house.

"Polly!" her mom shouted and enthusiastically hugged her the second after opening the door.

"Surprise!" Polly said. She returned the hug, then followed the tiny, blond woman inside.

She decided she would spend tonight with her parents and then surprise Grady tomorrow.

* * *

Polly parked the rental in a space in front of the large accounting firm where Grady worked. It was almost lunchtime so she would take him for a surprise lunch.

Polly: Are you back from your trip?
Grady: Yup. Hard at work.

She smiled and waited. Noon rolled around, and she saw several people stream out of the firm. No Grady, though. Maybe he brought lunch and was staying in.

She climbed out of the car and kept her head down as she walked up the sidewalk to the building. No one recognized her, and she successfully entered the doors without hesitation. A large reception desk sat in the lobby and a brunette receptionist sat behind it.

Polly smiled and approached her.

The receptionist smiled. "Hi, what can I do for you?"

"Hi, I'm looking for Grady McClelland."

The receptionist frowned. "I'm sorry, but he's not here."

"Oh, did he step out for lunch? Maybe I missed him walk by."

"No." She shook her head. "I haven't seen him in probably six months. Mr. McClelland is no longer employed here."

Polly's stomach sank, and she felt like she was going to be sick. "Oh, okay. I didn't know. Thank you."

"Sure thing. You okay, honey? You look a little green."

"I'm okay. Thank you."

Polly walked quickly out the door and to her car. She sat down and panicked, her breaths coming hard.

First, the house key didn't work and now this? Was Grady hiding something from her?

Her phone chimed right as she pulled out of the parking lot, but she didn't hear it.

She drove across town to their house and pulled into the driveway outside. In the daylight, she noticed that the grass in the front yard stood a little higher than normal. She also noticed something else she'd failed to see last night: a large realtor "for sale" sign in the middle of the lawn.

What the fuck?

Polly's heart beat wildly in her chest. What was he hiding? There was no reason for this. She'd offered to pay off this house with her first payment from the record label, but Grady had refused, saying he wanted to work for it and would make the mortgage payments. If he'd simply said something, she would have paid for the house in a heartbeat.

She pulled out her phone and dialed Grady.

"Hey, Pol," he said. "Good to hear from you. How are you?"

"Hey, I'm peachy. How are you?" she choked out.

"Great. I got back this morning from my work trip. Grinding away at the office."

A lie. Polly winced and swallowed. She could feel tears brimming and holding them back made her throat ache, but she willed them not to break free.

She said, "I got an unexpected break and I'm in town. How about I swing by the house tonight and make dinner?"

"Oh umm. Let's go out for dinner tonight and make plans. That way we can both relax and not have to worry about groceries or cleanup or anything."

That made sense...

"Where do you want to meet?"

Grady rattled off the restaurant information and planned to meet her there at 5:30. After he got off from work.

"Okay, see you later. Love you," he said.

"Love you, too."

"Bye."

"Bye."

She hung up the phone and sniffled. She looked up at the red brick home Grady had sworn would always be theirs. For sale.

She drew a deep breath and swallowed. Okay. Maybe there was an explanation. Maybe he'd changed jobs and bought a new house. Hard for her to believe, but maybe.

Polly sniffled and started the car with resignation. She would give him the benefit of the doubt and let him explain before she jumped to conclusions.

* * *

Polly pulled the rental car into a parking spot at the restaurant Grady picked and shifted to park. The restaurant looked like a nice Italian place from the outside, but Polly had never been, so she didn't know.

She climbed out of the car and smoothed the creases from her purple sundress. She grabbed her clutch purse from the passenger seat and closed the door.

She didn't see Grady's car yet, but she went inside.

She smiled at the hostess. "Hi, my name's Polly. I'm supposed to meet someone here. I'm not sure if he's here yet or not, but if he's not then I'd like to get a table."

"What's the name?" she asked.

"Grady McClelland."

"Ah, yes, miss. He's already here." The hostess grabbed a menu and gestured for Polly to follow her.

They approached a table toward the back, where Grady studied the menu. Polly found his familiar look comforting. He looked like he always did with his blond hair, glasses, and suit. Nothing seemed different.

He smiled and stood when he noticed them. Always courteous. "Hi, Polly," he said, stepping around the table to assist with her chair. She sat and thanked them both.

The hostess left and Grady sat down. He adjusted his glasses and spoke to her with excitement. "It's been so long since I saw you. You look better than ever, Polly. You got some sun on that beach."

"I did. Thank you," she said. She picked up the menu and fiddled with it.

"It's a pleasant surprise that you got an unplanned vacation."

"I know. A venue cancelled because a pipe burst, so I'm off until Saturday."

"That's great. Where are you planning on staying?"

She narrowed her eyes at him, but answered normally. "I planned to spend time with you so I'll stay at our place."

His eyes widened. "Oh, I wish you'd called first."

"Why?"

"I'm having it fumigated right now. A neighbor has a roach problem and I want to keep them out of the house. They said it would take several days to ensure the fumes leave."

Her heart sank. Another lie.

She noticed nothing unusual about his expression. He almost looked like he believed he spoke the truth.

"Where are you staying? A hotel? I'll stay with you," she said.

He shook his head. "I'm crashing on a buddy's couch."

"Then let's rent a hotel room together. I want to spend as much time with you as I can while I'm here."

"My buddy's actually moving, and I said I'd help. It'll be easiest if I stay there. I promised him and all."

Every word made her stomach upset. She felt the telltale gurgle and swallowed, trying to hold back the vomit.

She swallowed hard and said, "Oh. Well, if it's that big of an inconvenience... I can stay with my parents."

He nodded. "That may be best."

Her heart dropped. She cleared her throat. "How was your work trip?"

"Great! David gave a big presentation and got a huge pat on the back from Martin when we got back. I have to do a huge project for Mr. McDaniels now that we're back and it will take a lot of time." Grady reached across the table and grabbed her hand. "I've missed you. I love you."

Nausea overwhelmed her; she tried to keep it under control. He was lying. She knew because all the people he named worked at his old office, the one that said he no longer worked there.

"Grady. I—"

A shout interrupted them and a plate of spaghetti plastered against the front of Grady's shirt. Polly pulled her hand from Grady's and watched a young, dark-haired man, who she'd seen working as a server earlier, shout at Grady.

"How dare you? I knew there was a reason I never liked you!" the man shouted.

Grady's face went ashen. "Mark, it's not —"

"It is what it looks like!" The man turned to Polly. "Who is he to you?"

She swallowed. "Umm. Grady is my fiancée."

"See!?" The man turned back to Grady. "You're such an asshole."

"What's going on?" A man who appeared to be the manager asked, walking up to their table.

"This slimeball is married to my sister. Since college. They have three beautiful kids, and here he is on a date with his fiancée!"

The man pulled out his wallet and flashed a professional family portrait of Grady smiling with a woman and three kids.

Polly's gaze landed on Grady, who watched her with wide eyes. Her eyes flicked to his hand. A barely noticeable tan line where a wedding ring would be.

Her eyes filled with tears.

"Is this true?" she asked.

"No, Polly, I —"

"No?" the young man scoffed. "I was the best man at your wedding! I gave your oldest son a piggyback ride last night after your wife — my sister — fed us family dinner. Look at this picture." He waved his wallet in front of Grady's face then showed Polly the picture of the happy family. "It's true."

Tears spilled down Polly's cheeks.

She sobbed, "Mark, I'm sorry. Grady and I have been together for years. Since high school. I never knew he got married. I would never. Grady, fuck you. We're done. I expect all my shit back. Leave it with my parents."

She slid her engagement ring from her finger and placed it on the table, then stood and ran away.

"Polly," Grady shouted.

She heard him stand and start to follow. Then she heard chatter and saw cameras flashing.

Polly grabbed a menu off a table, opened it, and obscured the side of her face with it. She hoped that would ruin most of the paparazzi pictures. Who had told them she would be there anyway? She rushed out of the restaurant, tears flowing readily. Polly tore open the door on the rental and scrambled in. She tossed the menu on the passenger seat. Quickly, she peeled out of the parking lot. She left behind Grady and the paparazzi.

Polly sobbed so hard she had to pull over a few miles down the road because the tears blurred her vision to the point that she couldn't see.

Grady's infidelity devastated her. Yes, she'd gone away to college and toured with the band, which left him alone a lot — but they visited and talked on the phone as often as possible. He'd promised commitment and said he would wait as long as it took. She'd believed him. But Grady had a whole second life that she knew nothing about. She'd planned to marry that man... but he already had a wife and kids. A beautiful family. She'd seen the picture.

Her stomach heaved and she barely pushed the car door open before she puked all over the berm.

Polly closed the door. She wiped her mouth with her hand and sobbed. Overwhelmed, she sat there and cried for what seemed like hours but was probably only minutes.

Finally, she wiped her nose, took a deep breath, and put on her brave face. She had to get through this.

Where could she go? Her parents couldn't see her like this so she couldn't go there. They thought she was staying the night with Grady, anyway.

Polly shifted to drive and went to a hotel on the edge of town. She pulled into the parking lot and was about to get out of the car when her phone rang. She dug through her clutch to find it, accepted the call, and put it to her ear without even seeing who called.

"Hello?" she asked on the last ring.

"Polly, hey," Flynn's deep voice rumbled in her ear. "I saw the news. Are you okay?"

"What do you mean?"

"Grady."

Their fight made the news already?

She said, "You know the news exaggerates. I'm sure whatever they said was only half true."

"Uhh... Grady. Spaghetti. Secret life. Kids."

She sucked in a breath and the tears welled up again. The news got the main facts right for once. Usually they mangled reality and fiction together.

"Shit."

"Hey, hey, hey. It's okay. It'll blow over. We'll get shitfaced together and pretend this never happened," he said. "It's okay. I never liked that guy, anyway."

She sob-laughed. "You're the second person to say that tonight."

"With good reason. He's a sleaze. Good riddance. What do you need?"

"I don't know."

"Company? I'll come to you if you want."

Polly shook her head. "No, I'll be okay. Stay on tour."

"Where are you?"

"I'm okay," she repeated. "I'll check into a hotel tonight."

"You need moral support. I don't want you to be alone. Can you go visit a friend?"

Polly refused to impose on anyone by dropping in like that. She wasn't close enough to anyone here to do that, anyway.

"Flynn, I'm not doing that. I'm okay."

"Hmmm." He paused. "Do you promise me you're okay?"

"Yes."

She heard him shift on the other side of the phone. "I still don't think you should be alone."

"Flynn, I'm okay. I promise."

He sighed and remained silent for a moment then seemed to reach a decision. "Fine. I'll accept your promise and won't track your phone's location. For now. What's your answer to my question?"

"What question?"

"I texted you earlier. Go to the Synergic Awards ceremony in California with me in two days? As friends? I need a date."

"Two days? The dresses for those ceremonies can take two years." She didn't have any dresses worthy of a fancy awards ceremony.

"Two days. Wear jeans, I don't care. Say yes."

"Jeans. You're going to regret saying that," she said with a laugh.

"No, I'm not. Go with me." She could hear his smile.

"Okay. When you're in a tux and I'm in jeans, it'll serve you right."

"Yes?"

"Yes."

"Yes!" he shouted in the background. She could picture the fist-pump he did, too. "I'll email you the details."

"Okay. Is there a dress code?"

"I don't think so."

He cleared his throat and his voice grew serious. "Wanna do a movie night tonight?" he asked.

"But you're across the country."

"I know. You put me on speaker, we turn on the same movie, and we watch it together. Through the phone. Even though we're on opposite coasts."

"That... Would probably work. You want to do that?"

"I do."

Polly knew what he was doing — she wouldn't let him physically come to her, so he was trying everything in his power to make sure she wasn't alone. The bad boy rocker, "with no heart" as his fans said, was trying to be a good friend.

"It's like 3 pm there," she said.

"All the better to watch a movie," he said. "It's early enough and I'm sober enough, I'll remember the details."

She laughed. "Okay. I'm going to check into the hotel and take a shower. Call me back in like an hour."

"Promise you'll answer."

"I promise. Pick a good movie."

"Deal," he said and disconnected the call.

She glanced at her phone and chuckled. Flynn had indeed texted her earlier about the ceremony. She texted back: *Jeans :)*

She thumbed through her other unread messages. Members of the band asking what really happened and if she was okay. She sent quick responses to them. When she reached the multiple messages from Grady, she deleted them and blocked his number.

TABLOID NEWS
"HOMEWRECKER"

In breaking news, Lovely Oblivion guitarist Polly Worthington turns out to be a homewrecker. The guitarist reportedly engaged in a relationship with Grady McClelland, a married man with multiple children, despite knowing of Mr. McClelland's family. Ms. Worthington reportedly blatantly did not care about his other relationship. Mr. McClelland's brother-in-law uncovered the affair when Mr. McClelland escorted Ms. Worthington to a local restaurant on a date. Despite Mr. McClelland's lengthy marriage, Ms. Worthington does not appear remorseful about ending it and said, "I'm sorry. We've been together for years."

Witnesses report that Mr. McClelland's relationships with both Mrs. McClelland and Ms. Worthington are terminated at this time. Ms. Worthington loved and left, leaving Mr. McClelland's house broken and devastated. More on this story later.

Chapter 4
Polly

The hot water flowed over her body, the scent of the hotel's complimentary rosemary mint shampoo filling her nostrils.

Tears flooded her eyes again, and she sniffled. Turning her face into the water, she wiped them away. She'd dated Grady since sophomore year of high school. Over ten years with the man, all gone. She'd only ever been with him. Always faithful, always loyal. Pointlessly.

Reality hit her. That chapter of her life was closed — and she'd wasted it on Grady.

She'd spent so many years of her life on Grady, and he simply threw them away to create a second life behind her back.

She crumpled onto the floor of the shower and sobbed against her knees.

Why her? She'd never cheated on him. Never even kissed another man.

Polly cried on the floor of the shower until the water ran cold. The cold water was the equivalent of a slap in the face. How long had she been in there to run a hotel's hot water tank cold? She stood and turned off the water. She shivered and dried her hair, then wrapped a towel around herself.

She opened the door and walked into her room, which was freezing. She crossed the soft carpet and turned off the air conditioner, immediately making a difference.

She laid down on the bed and picked up her phone. She had a missed call from Flynn and a voicemail.

Polly pressed the button to listen to the message.

Flynn's voice came through loud and clear. *I assume you're still in the shower. You've had a big day and you're sorting it out. I get it. I'm calling you back in 30 minutes. If you don't answer then, I'm calling in reinforcements. I don't know what that means, but*

I'll do it if I have to. But I won't have to because you're going to answer next time I call. Right? Talk to you soon.

Polly half laughed and checked the time. Thirty minutes had passed since his voicemail.

Right on time, the phone rang in her hand. A photo of Flynn's mischievous face filled the screen.

"Hello," she said, as she answered the call.

"Why hello there. Thank you for answering."

She sighed and slid her body under the covers. "I'm sorry. My shower took longer than I thought."

"I figured. Are you okay?"

"I will be."

"I'm here if you need to talk. Standing offer."

"Thank you."

His voice deepened. He adopted a tour guide tone. "Okay, now turn your attention to Spike TV. We're going to watch 'Shooter,' starring Mr. Mark Wahlberg, formerly known as Marky Mark, which comes on in five minutes."

She grabbed the remote and changed the channel, which showed commercials. She settled back against the pillows to wait.

"The channel's on."

"Okay, put me on speaker," he instructed.

Polly hit the button on her phone and put it on the pillow by her head.

"Can you hear me?" she asked.

"Loud and clear. Can you hear me?"

"Yes, Master Flynn."

He huffed a laugh. "Okay, good."

They watched the movie together over the phone, laughing and making comments about the show, until finally she fell asleep.

* * *

Flynn

Flynn would recognize that makeup-less face anywhere. The blond he waited for entered the baggage area at the airport, her hat pulled low and her face unmarked to keep recognition down.

He whistled to catch her attention, and her eyes shot to him. He smiled, pulling his own hat low but flashing a dimple at her. She nodded acknowledgement.

He approached her, knocked her playfully with his hip, and helped grab her bag.

"Hey," he said simply.

"Hey," she responded with a smile.

They left the airport as fast as possible, before one of them was spotted. He led her to the inconspicuous black town car in the parking lot and they ducked into the backseat.

"Let's go back to the hotel," Flynn told the driver, who nodded and began driving.

Flynn turned his gaze to Polly. "Did you bring your camera?"

"I did."

Flynn nodded. "Good. Can you take some pics at the award show for me?"

Polly smiled. "Sure."

"Awesome. Also, we're going out later."

"You going to elaborate?"

"Nope. When do you have to be back?"

"I have to be in Richmond on Saturday morning."

He nodded. "It's what, Wednesday? I've got..." He mentally calculated. "Until Friday before I have to be back on the bus. I can probably make that Saturday if I fly instead. I'll play it by ear."

"The awards show is tonight?"

Flynn nodded. "Yes. Then after that, you and I are going out."

She frowned. "What does that mean?"

"You'll see."

"Not helpful."

Flynn laughed. "I've never pretended to be helpful."

Polly shook her head. "Fine. Keep your secret. What award are you guys up for, anyway?"

"Late Nyght Smoke got nominated for Song of the Year at the Synergic Awards."

"Awesome. That's a big deal."

Flynn smiled. "We got nominated, but I don't expect a win. Still, it's an honor for the nomination."

"But what if you do win? Won't the band want you to celebrate?"

He flashed her a dimple. "They'll go without me. I have other plans."

"I don't want to keep you from a celebration."

"Don't worry about it. I want to spend tonight with you. After the ceremony, it's you and me. Nothing's changing my mind."

Their car pulled to the curb at the front entrance of a hotel. Flynn glanced around outside and when he saw the coast was clear. He donned sunglasses, grabbed her duffle bag, and climbed from the car.

Flynn hooped around the vehicle and reached for Polly's hand. She took it, and together they walked from the car into the hotel, gazes down, attempting to look inconspicuous.

Flynn led them into the hotel elevator and hit the button for their floor. When the door slid closed, he finally looked up.

"You ready to have a fantastic time and forget all about your ex?" He squeezed her hand.

"I wish I could forget him. Unfortunately, that's impossible."

Flynn shoved his sunglasses on top of his head and squinted at her. "Why?"

"I was with Grady since high school. He got all my important firsts. I..." She shifted uncomfortably. "I've only ever been with Grady. He'll always be in my memories."

Flynn let go of her hand to wrap an arm around her shoulders and pull her against his side in a half hug. He kissed her temple. He couldn't deny that those words made him feel unexpectedly possessive.

She had only been with one man... He couldn't relate. He knew she wouldn't want to hear the tally of how many women he'd been with. Though he'd slowed down now, Flynn had fully embraced the rockstar lifestyle when his band first hit it big: he'd taken the "sex, drugs, and rock and roll" motto to heart. But after several years of drugs and one-night-stands, Flynn grew tired of that lifestyle and it was no longer his norm. That kind of loyalty, her loyalty, felt as rare and exotic as a unicorn to him. As much of a treasure.

"Loyalty is fine. Admirable even," he said. "Don't compare every man to him. He's a douche canoe. Everyone's different. Loyalty is a fantastic trait. The right guy will want it. He'll help you make new memories. Better ones. I'll help you find a good partner."

"Really?"

He squeezed her shoulders and smiled at her. "Of course. If you haven't noticed, I consider you my close friend. Honestly, you're probably my best friend. I definitely need to screen your dates. I don't get along with everyone. I can't have my dear friend's boyfriend hating me. How else will I know he and I are compatible?"

Her laughter made him smile.

They both glanced ahead as the elevator opened on their floor.

She walked forward first, out of his reach. He dropped his arm to his side and stepped from the elevator. They walked together down the hotel hallway to their room, which he opened with a card key.

The door opened to a standard double hotel room, with two queen-sized beds.

Polly laid on one of the beds. Flynn set her duffle bag on its foot then laid down on the empty bed.

"I see your clothes are here already," she said. She gestured toward his tux bag hanging in the closet.

"Yeah, that's what my manager told me to wear."

"Interesting."

He laughed. "I don't like how you say that," he said.

"You'll look great."

He chuffed. "Again. Not liking your words."

Swiftly, she changed the subject. "What are we doing after the ceremony?"

"Having fun."

Even though he wasn't looking at her, he knew she rolled her eyes hard. He could almost hear them. He smiled to himself.

"Relax. We'll play it by ear," he said.

Flynn's phone chimed, and he pulled it from his pocket. A text from his manager.

"How do you feel about heading out early? My manager wants an interview done at a radio station before the ceremony," he said.

"That's fine with me. You can get ready first if you want."

"Okay, cool."

He climbed out of bed, grabbed his tux, and disappeared into the bathroom. Quickly, Flynn showered, dressed in his tux which was complete with a bowtie, and ran his hands through his hair to spike it.

He walked out of the bathroom adjusting his cuffs. He smiled when he heard the tell-tale "click". Flynn looked up and Polly sat on her bed holding her camera.

"You look great in a tux," she said and snapped another picture.

He grinned at her and she snapped another.

"Thank you. I'll model for you anytime," he said. "Bathroom's all yours."

She set her camera on the bed and grabbed her duffle bag.

"Be right back."

She disappeared into the bathroom. Flynn sat down at the room's table and thumbed through social media on his phone.

He heard the shower and the blow dryer. Polly stepped out of the bathroom, her makeup on point and her hair styled into her stage look of space buns. He laughed when he saw her clothing. She wore dark jeans and a nice blue blouse, complete with matching sapphire earrings and necklace.

"You weren't lying about the jeans."

She smiled. "I was not. I told you multiple times."

She walked over and set her duffle bag on her bed.

"Now I feel overdressed."

"I told you."

Flynn smirked. "You did. Okay, picture time."

"What?" She laughed.

"As a pair, we look ridiculous. Let's get a picture so we have this memory for later. I'll change before we leave so I match the psychopath I'm escorting. You'll be the only one to see this, and I know you'll want a picture. Now's your chance, picture lady."

"Really?"

He quirked an eyebrow. "Polly."

"Okay, okay."

Polly grabbed her camera off the bed and set up the timer. She set it on the table and looked through the lens to make sure the angle was right, then she scurried into place.

"Right here," she said.

Flynn swooped in, grinned at the camera, and tucked an arm around Polly. Her vanilla scent filled his nose, bringing images of warmth and comfort to him. The flash went off, the camera taking their picture, and he blinked as he pulled back.

"Okay, I just need a sec then we can go," he said.

"I'm ready when you are."

He went to the closet, rummaged through his bag, and grabbed a couple of items. He turned and smiled at a devious-looking Polly then disappeared into the bathroom.

Flynn tugged his bowtie undone and smirked at his reflection. Leave it to Polly to change the rules. His manager would have a fit. But damn, would it be worth it to see the look on his face. Flynn took off his tux and put on his nicest jeans and a button-up gray shirt. He rolled the shirt sleeves to his elbows, which showed off his tattooed sleeves. The business casual attire looked good, but it was no tux.

He stepped from the bathroom, and Polly whistled when she saw him.

She approached, wrapped her hands around his collar, and straightened his shirt.

"Lookin' sharp, Flynn. I like this better than the tux."

She looked up at him and smiled, smoothing her hands over the front of his shirt.

Flynn gazed down at her hazel eyes. His breath hitched when she beamed at him. The trust in her expression floored him. No one else looked at him with full appreciation and faith. In his mind, he knew she was beautiful, but in that moment he could only see her beauty.

For the first time, he wondered if he and Polly could be "more" than friends. His eyes flicked to her lips. Why hadn't he considered it before?

He tucked a strand of hair behind her ear as he remembered. The timing wasn't right. He'd firmly placed her in the friend zone and never looked back when they met. Probably because she'd been engaged and he knew he didn't have a chance. And now she was coming off a breakup.

Polly patted his chest and picked a piece of lint off his shirt, snapping him from his train of thought.

He smiled nervously and cleared his throat, which suddenly seemed dry. "You about ready?"

"Yes. I'll grab my purse and we can go."

Polly walked to her bed and grabbed a small crossbody bag from her duffle. She stuffed her wallet, phone, and camera in then placed the strap over her shoulder.

"I'm ready."

Flynn texted the driver that they were on the way. He opened the door, and they walked into the hallway. He clasped her hand in his, and they headed downstairs toward the car.

Chapter 5
Polly

"Dude, Miguel is going to murder you," Flynn's drummer, Zack, said with a laugh, referencing the band's manager, Miguel. The long-haired drummer offered a hand to Flynn, and they did a complicated handshake. Zack and the three other members of Late Nyght Smoke stood in the hallway at the radio station wearing tuxes. None of the band appeared surprised about the outfits, although their dates seemed disgusted.

"Nah," Flynn said. "He'll enjoy the extra press."

Flynn looked business casual compared to the rest of his band, who wore formal.

The band introduced their dates to Polly and Flynn. The women all screamed "groupie" to Polly, and she didn't attempt to remember their names. They all wore fashionable outfits and dressed to the nines.

They all stood in the hallway, listening to the light sounds of the radio station that played over some overhead speakers.

The middle-aged, average looking DJ went on commercial break and opened the studio door to wave the band inside. Polly and the rest of the dates stayed in the hall. She watched them get seated and adjust microphones through the glass viewing wall of the hallway.

Polly pulled out her camera and took a few behind-the-scenes snapshots as they settled in.

A sign that read "on the air" turned on in the window.

Polly heard the DJ's voice come over the building's speakers. She could see his mouth moving inside, but could only hear the radio broadcast over the speakers. She also noticed a small lag between reality and the broadcast.

"Thanks for joining us here today," the announcer said. "I understand you've been nominated for Song of the Year."

"Yes," the lead singer, Will, answered. He tucked his blond hair behind his ear. "A nomination is an honor itself. We would be humbled if we win that category. We have the greatest fans and we're only here because of them."

The DJ chatted with them and asked the standard interview questions for a while.

Soon he asked, "Who is that out there in the hallway?"

"Who?" Will asked.

"The woman that looks familiar."

Flynn cleared his throat. "She's with me. That's my good friend, Polly. She's accompanying me to the awards ceremony tonight."

"Is that Polly of Lovely Oblivion?"

"Yes, sir."

"Are we seeing a relationship bud? Are there little Polynn mixes in the works?"

Polly started laughing. Polynn? "Pollen"? What an awful name.

Flynn's hand hit his face, and he shook his head. "Please don't mash our names like that. Polly and I are good friends. That's it. Nothing to tell."

Polly laughed so hard her knees buckled and she crumpled onto the floor. Her laughter continued. The other women looked at her like she was insane.

"Well," the DJ said. "Since Polly is dying of laughter in my hallway, I'm inclined to believe you."

Flynn chuckled. "You should. We aren't together. And now I'll never hear the end of this Polynn thing and how her name came first, so thanks."

The DJ chuckled. "Why are you both dressed in jeans? Didn't you say you're attending the awards? I mean, you look nice but the rest of your band is in formal wear. Don't you feel a little underdressed?"

Flynn laughed. "We're both in jeans because my companion doesn't follow social norms. I'm humoring her. I don't care what outfits we wear."

"Well, there you have it, listeners. Look for their 'small town dress-up' on the carpet today." The DJ laughed. "Thanks for stopping by, guys. I'm here today with Late Nyght Smoke. Are there plans to release new music anytime soon?"

Zack leaned forward and spoke. "We can't give the date yet, but new music is coming soon. Follow us on social media for official updates."

"You heard it here first, folks. Keep an ear out for upcoming releases from Late Nyght Smoke."

The broadcast cut to commercials.

Polly sat on the floor with her back against the wall. She pressed a hand to her ribs, which hurt from laughing so hard.

Murmurs went around the group's dates about how she had obviously lost her mind to behave like that in front of such a prestigious band like Late Nyght Smoke. She laughed even harder because she knew all the band members — they were regular guys and would probably be on the floor, too, if they weren't on the air. Not only would she tease Flynn about the nickname, they would, too. They may be famous, but they were regular people, too.

The band filed from the broadcast room in their tuxes and picked up their dates. They winked or nodded at Polly. They headed outside to the car. Flynn followed last in his business casual, entering the hallway alone with Polly. He walked closer and knelt beside her.

"You okay down here?"

"Oh yes, Master Flynn. I'm peachy."

He pursed his lips and looked at her like it took all his effort to hold back a comment about peaches. She patted his cheek, and he smiled at her affectionately.

"Let's get out of here," she said.

He smiled. "Yes, ma'am."

Flynn stood and offered a hand to Polly to pull her to her feet. They linked arms and walked down the hallway, out the door to the waiting cars.

* * *

The band took two limos to the ceremony. Flynn and Polly waited until last to exit their car. They listened as one reporter announced each couple. "And here we have the lovely Zack of Late Nyght Smoke accompanied by his date..."

"Rochelle," the brunette said.

"Rochelle. Zack wears a traditional Armani tux, and Rochelle wears a Tina Zee original red dress with Jimmy Choo heels. Very nice ensembles."

Polly laughed from her spot beside Flynn. "I can't wait to hear how we're announced."

Flynn intertwined their fingers and squeezed. "I'm curious, too."

Flynn stepped through the door, and they climbed from the car. A concrete barrier formed a walkway to the building, and a crowd of paparazzi and screaming fans swarmed the boundary. Lights flashed as they took pictures.

Flynn and Polly shut the limo door and stood side by side, hands clasped.

"And here we have Flynn of Late Nyght Smoke with his date Polly of Lovely Oblivion. Both wear Levi's..."

The reporter's voice trailed off. Open-mouthed disbelief crossed her face. Obviously, in her mind, awards ceremonies were for showing off.

Flynn smirked at her and tugged Polly against his side. They posed for photos in front of a couple of cameras, then walked together to the sleek auditorium entrance with Flynn's arm around her.

Flynn's band gathered around a nearby bench, so they joined them. Their manager, Miguel, stood amongst them. A fedora hat covered his dark hair and his tux looked spot-on. He reminded

Polly of a movie mobster, and she almost expected to hear an east coast accent.

"Whoa, what the fuck, Flynn? That is not the tux I sent you," Miguel said.

Flynn squeezed Polly's shoulders. He subtly winked at her. He looked down at his clothes, his eyebrows wrinkled and a dumbfounded expression crossed his face. "What do you mean? I'm wearing what they delivered in the bag."

"I sent everyone in the band a tux for tonight."

Flynn shook his head. "I'm wearing what I got, Miguel. Polly had a beautiful ball gown on and I made her change to match. I thought we were all wearing business casual."

Miguel leveled an all-knowing look at Flynn. "You're a great actor, maybe almost as good at that as you are with a guitar, and I might have believed you — if I hadn't already heard your radio interview."

Flynn grinned. "Heard that, did you?"

"I did." Miguel sighed. "At least this'll bring extra publicity."

Flynn muttered in Zack's direction, "Ha! Told you."

"But do what I tell you from now on," Miguel said.

Flynn bit the inside of his cheek, holding back a laugh. "Whatever you say, sir."

Miguel rolled his eyes and turned back to the rest of the band. "Let's get good seats. You guys have a great shot at winning tonight. No matter what, you've got Song of the Year in my eyes."

The guys collectively groaned, but they and their dates followed Miguel into the auditorium. An usher showed them to their section. Polly sat a few seats from the end of the aisle. Before he left, the usher commented quietly, "I love your outfit. You look beautiful."

"Thank you." She smiled at him and whispered back, "No one's going to kick me out, are they?"

He grinned and patted her shoulder. "No. The organizers didn't issue an official dress code. You look great. Don't let anyone say you don't."

"Thank you."

He nodded. "You're welcome. Have fun." He disappeared up the aisle.

As they settled into their seats, Flynn tugged Polly's hand into his and squeezed.

"You okay?" he whispered.

"I'm good." She smiled at him.

Flynn flashed her his real smile — not the panty-dropping one he reserved for fans, but a genuine smile that reached his eyes. That made his next statement more special to her.

"Thank you for coming with me," he said. "It means the world to me that you're here."

"Sure thing. I've had fun."

"Good." He kissed the back of her hand. The unusual gesture struck Polly — Flynn had never done that before — but after her initial shock, the action seemed natural and quickly faded from Polly's mind.

They waited as more people filled the auditorium, some recognizable faces and some not.

Soon, the seat next to Polly's filled. A famous, handsome face grinned at her. The blond man extended his hand. "Hi, I'm Gideon Trent."

Gideon found fame in country music and his latest song hit #1 at the top of the country charts. His manager sat in the seat on his other side.

Polly smiled and shook Gideon's hand. "Polly Worthington."

"Ah, Lovely Oblivion." Gideon beamed. "Nice to meet you." Polly gave him a shocked look and he laughed. "Yeah, I perform country music, but don't be fooled. I listen to y'all, and I'm a big fan."

Polly blushed at the unexpected compliment. "Thank you."

Gideon nodded. "You're welcome. Does your band have a nomination today?"

"No, I'm here with a friend who does." Polly gestured over her shoulder. She flashed a smile at Flynn, who glared at them. "Flynn," she hissed and elbowed him.

Gideon glanced at Flynn, who scowled and ignored him. Gideon turned his attention back to Polly. "Well, I'm pleased to meet you, Ms. Polly. I'm surprised you aren't here for a nomination, but I'm sure glad to meet you."

"Thank you, you too. Congratulations on your nomination."

"Much appreciated," he said with a smile.

The overhead lights dimmed.

"Listen," Gideon said. He reached into his pocket, pulled out a card, and handed it to Polly. "This is my number. My cell is on there. Call me when you get a chance and we'll do lunch. I'd love to talk music with you."

"I will, thank you." Polly smiled at him and slipped his business card into her purse.

Polly knew her reaction screamed confidence, but inside she breathed a sigh of relief that they'd stopped talking. Grady's treatment shook her confidence.

Their attention shifted as a spotlight bathed the podium that sat mid-stage. Two large screens sat on the sides of the stage for the crowd's view.

The announcer, a well-known country artist, crossed to center stage and talked into his microphone.

"Good evening, everyone. Thank you for coming. We are here today to recognize some of the greatest musical talent in existence. To start us off, we have a performance from one of this country's favorite jazz bands."

The audience cheered and applauded before he even got the band name out.

"I see they need no introduction," he said with a laugh. "Enjoy."

Polly applauded and made the appropriate oohs and ahhs as the night progressed. She cheered for Gideon as he won his nomination and congratulated him when he returned to his seat.

Polly snapped candid pictures of the attendees and the awards. Her mind wandered freely, imagining the what-ifs of her future. The only part of her life set in stone was her record contract. Otherwise, she had no obligations and could do anything. Could someone like Gideon be in her future? Had she met her "forever" yet? Would she be good enough for him?

Unexpectedly, Gideon and his manager stood. Before he left, Gideon whispered, "I'm sorry. I got an emergency message. I have to leave. It was nice to meet you. Call me, okay?"

Polly frowned. "Okay. I hope everything is all right."

He shook his head. "I hope so, but I don't know. Take care."

"Thanks, you too."

Quickly, Gideon and his manager exited. They left behind empty seats.

Polly's thoughts drifted again.

When Flynn gripped her hand and bounced his knee restlessly, she squeezed his hand and focused back on the announcer. Flynn pulled her hand to his lips and mumbled something against it. She couldn't hear the words, but she assumed he prayed.

Flynn put up a front and acted like this award was no big deal, when really it could do wonders for his band.

"...and now for Song of the Year."

Clips of the nominees' music videos played on the screens.

Tension filled the room as the videos played and the announcer waited to tell them who won. Flynn's grin stood out to Polly on the screen as his band's video played.

The announcer drew out his speech but finally he said, "Our winner is... Late Nyght Smoke for *What It Means*."

The band jumped from their chairs and cheered. Polly leapt up and hugged Flynn.

"Congratulations, Flynn!"

"Thank you!"

Flynn leaned in and his eyes flicked to her mouth as his lips grew closer. Polly's heart thudded and butterflies of anticipation fluttered in her stomach. Was Flynn really going to kiss her?

At the last second, though, his lips touched her cheek. Unexpectedly, disappointment flooded her, but she forced a smile and congratulated him. How strange. She'd never had feelings other than friendship for Flynn. She was sure he didn't have other feelings than friendship for her.

Polly stepped out of the way and clapped as the band filed from their seats, congratulating each of them as they passed her on their walk to the stage.

She settled in her chair and thought about this new development. She watched Flynn's handsome grin as the band stepped up to the podium. He glanced at her and winked. She'd always known he looked good, but seeing him on that stage increased his appeal. That hard, chiseled body and panty-melting smile... For the first time since Grady, Polly had scandalous thoughts about someone. The fact that they were about Flynn surprised her. Could she and Flynn be "more" or would it ruin their friendship? Would he want to be more?

The band accepted their plaques with a huge shout out to the fans, and their lead singer, Will, gave a gracious speech on their behalf. "Thanks for your help in achieving this award. We can use all the help we can get so we're lucky that our fans are the best," he said. Camera flashes filled the room, and they held their poses for a minute to let the paparazzi finish. Polly got a great photo of the band and their awards for Flynn; she knew he'd want it.

Before she knew it, the guys were back in their seats and Flynn's warm body pressed into the spot next to hers.

"Congrats again," she whispered.

"Thanks." He showed her the impressive plaque. "Song of the Year" blazed in big, bold letters across the award and a metal plate printed the band name underneath.

"Pretty sweet," she said.

"Definitely. This is going on the wall in my studio. I'm fucking proud because I wrote that song. I never expected it to get Song of the Year." Flynn grinned then held the award toward her. "Can you stick this in your purse for me?"

"Sure."

Polly tucked Flynn's award carefully into her purse.

They finished watching the ceremony and clapped along when needed. After the last award went out and the audience started dispersing, Miguel stood and turned to the band.

"I have tickets to an exclusive after-party for you guys. I expect all of you to attend."

"Can't. Polly and I have plans," Flynn said.

Miguel frowned. "You won a big award, now is the time to network."

"We can't. Sorry. See ya." Flynn flashed him a smirk that looked less-than-sorry.

Flynn stood from his seat, grabbed Polly's hand, and ran. He pulled her with him. Polly heard Miguel shout Flynn's name. They dodged people in the aisle, ran around other attendees, and exited the building quickly through a side door. They avoided the press and slipped out unnoticed.

Outside on the sidewalk, Flynn entwined her fingers in his. He laughed and pulled his phone from his pocket with his other hand.

"Well, that was a rush," Flynn said.

"Yeah. Miguel will be pissed," Polly said.

"I don't care. I refuse to spend tonight at an after-party. I rarely get to see you. I want to do something else," he said.

Polly laughed. "Whatever you say, Master Flynn."

They continued walking. When they were a block away from the auditorium, Flynn led her to sit on a bench, then used his app to order an Uber for them. Once the Uber order was complete, he shoved his phone into his pocket.

"It's freezing," Polly commented about the cool night. Goosebumps raised on her arms.

"I'm sorry. I don't have a jacket. Come here."

Flynn put his arm over the back of the bench and wrapped it around her shoulders as they sat in the cool night air. They watched the traffic pass by on the night-time city street.

She relaxed and settled into his side. He wrapped his arm tighter and pulled her close. Wrapped in a warm Flynn cocoon, she sighed contently, rested her head on his shoulder, and enjoyed being with him like this. His warm coffee scent filled her senses.

Flynn felt like comfort to her, and she wanted to enjoy that as much as possible. They'd have to separate in a few days and she probably wouldn't see him until Boston. They both traveled so much with work.

Her heart beat a little faster when she thought about what it would be like to belong to Flynn, to be this close to him whenever she wanted for no reason, but she quickly shoved that thought away. Friends. She couldn't risk losing what they had, especially if he didn't feel the same.

"What do you want to do tonight?" he asked. He squeezed her shoulder.

"Whatever you want. I don't have a preference."

Flynn was quiet for a minute. They waited on the bench and simply listened to the quiet sounds around them: the wind rustling, the engines and tires on nearby roads, the distant laughter.

He rested his chin on her head.

"I owe you a night of getting shitfaced. Want to close out a bar?" he asked.

"You want to stay out all night drinking?"

He chuckled. "Yes. "

Polly laughed. "Okay."

He kissed her hair. "I've got this. Trust me. We'll have fun."

"Okay, Master Flynn." She snuggled into his warmth as they waited for the Uber.

TABLOID NEWS
"Smoke and Oblivion Escorted Out"

In breaking news, Late Nyght Smoke guitarist Flynn Morgan showed up at the Synergic Music Awards with Lovely Oblivion guitarist Polly Worthington, both defiantly wearing jeans to a formal event. Late Nyght Smoke was nominated for, and won, Song of the Year. Despite a strict dress code, both Polly and Flynn wore jeans. Reportedly, this was Polly's idea in protest of Lovely Oblivion's recently cancelled tour stop. Both were escorted from the premises before the show concluded because of violation of dress code and were denied entrance to the exclusive after-party. Rumor has it Flynn got into a fistfight at the party's door when the guard denied them access.

Chapter 6
Polly

The Uber pulled up to the curb in front of Caesar's Bar, a run down dive in the city where the C no longer lit up on the sign of the small brick building. The building sat nestled between other businesses on the small side street.

"This place is the best," Flynn said. "Thanks, man." He nodded at the Uber driver and they climbed from the car.

Polly grabbed the back of Flynn's shirt, and he led her inside.

The small bar had booths lining one wall and a long bar top lining the other. It was dim and dingy, but many people were present, which probably meant it was popular.

Flynn walked to the end of the bar furthest from the door, and they sat on barstools. He flagged down the bartender.

"Can I have a whiskey sour?" he asked.

"A sex on the beach, please?" she asked.

The gruff looking male bartender nodded and said, "Sure." He walked away to mix their drinks.

"If you wanted sex on the beach, you should've said something. I would've changed our plans," Flynn teased.

Polly laughed. *Like that would ever be an option.*

"I'll stick with the drink right now. I might need a few of them to work up to the actual act later, but I'll keep you posted," she teased back.

She glanced at Flynn in time to see him suck in a breath and swallow hard. He looked away from her. He cleared his throat and returned her gaze, though he seemed awkward.

"Drink up," he said with an awkward half smile. "I promised you we'd get shitfaced. No one here will call the reporters."

The bartender slid their drinks in front of them. "Enjoy."

They clinked their drinks together and toasted.

"To happiness and health," Flynn said.

"Happiness and health. Cheers."

Flynn drank a couple gulps of his whiskey sour. "That's good," he said. He made an appreciative face and set it down.

Polly took a sip of her drink. "Mmm fruity. And strong. Another of these and I'll be tipsy."

"That's okay. Drink up. You're safe, I've got you." He smiled softly at her, and warm trust washed over Polly. Flynn would keep his word.

Polly and Flynn spent the night hanging out at the bar, drinking, laughing, dancing, and having a great time.

At closing, they drunkenly stumbled into a waiting Uber, singing pirate songs. Daylight had already broken the sky.

"A pirate's life for me!" Polly belted, then she and Flynn giggled.

"Captain, ahoy!" Flynn said to the Uber driver as he buckled his seatbelt. "Take us to where we might find rations."

The long-haired surfer-looking driver shook his head and responded, "You booked me to take you to a diner a few blocks from here. Those rations still sound good?"

"Oh yeah. Diner. Bacon. Mmm. Aye, captain. Sail there," Flynn answered.

The driver laughed and pulled away from the curb.

Polly candidly snapped the driver's profile photo, then tucked her camera back in her purse.

"What was that for?" Flynn asked.

"Memories."

Flynn smiled. "Cool. Send me copies, too, would you?"

She gave him a small smile. "Okay."

Within a few minutes, the car pulled up to the curb outside a nondescript diner named Lou's. Flynn slipped their driver a cash tip as they climbed from the car. "Thanks, man," Polly heard him say.

Together, they stumbled into the building. When they opened the door, the scent of eggs and bacon hit Polly's nose.

"Hello," a cheery young server called out to them. "Would you like a table?"

"Yes, please," Polly responded.

To Polly's relief, the server seated them at a table toward the back of the restaurant, away from the windows.

Flynn ordered a black coffee and breakfast without looking at the menu. Polly couldn't help but notice he didn't have his glasses with him. He acted like a pro, ordering something available at every restaurant, like he already knew the menu. She ordered orange juice and blueberry pancakes. The server left them with reassurances that she would be back with their food soon. She didn't acknowledge their drunkenness.

Polly laid her hands on the table, then put her chin on them. She looked at Flynn.

"This diner... Good idea," she said.

"Yeah. I think we..." Hiccup. "...may have had a little much to drink. Need to soak up some of the booze."

Flynn reached across the table and trailed his fingers down Polly's cheek. He smiled, and Polly loved that it touched his eyes.

"Beautiful," he said.

She grinned. "Thank you. You look awesome, too."

His fingers coiled a strand of her hair, his thumb running over the texture.

Her heart thudded a little faster as he opened his mouth to speak. Right then, the server arrived with their food. Flynn released her hair and sat back.

Polly wasn't sure what she expected, but disappointment hit her.

A plate of blueberry pancakes and a bottle of maple syrup appeared in front of Polly. Biscuits and gravy, eggs, and bacon appeared before Flynn.

"Thank you," he said to the server.

"You're welcome, honey. If you need anything else, let me know." She flashed them a smile and left.

"Mmm bacon," Flynn muttered before digging in. They met eyes, and they both snickered.

Polly poured syrup on her pancakes and took a bite. The fluff and blueberry flavor hit her tongue. She washed it down with a sip of orange juice and moaned as the intense flavor exploded in her mouth. Best food ever.

"You like?" Flynn asked.

"Very much." She nodded. "I'm homeless. I may move in here. I wonder what they'd charge for rent."

Flynn laughed at her joke, then he grew serious and locked gazes with her.

"What do you mean, homeless?" he asked.

"Oh sorry, I thought I told you. Grady cleared out our house and there's a for sale sign in the yard. He didn't even tell me. I tried to go home right before we broke up and the locks are changed. I have to find a new place to live." She shrugged like Grady's betrayal hadn't hurt her.

He shook his head no. "Whoa, what the fuck? That's insane." He added ketchup to his plate. "Anyway, you're not homeless. You can stay with me."

Her heart skipped a beat, and she swallowed hard. She would love to, but she couldn't. It was too dangerous for their friendship.

"I don't know if that's a good idea. We're drunk."

"I'm only a little buzzed. It makes sense. We can have movie night every night when we're both home. There's space for a darkroom. You'll have your own bedroom and bathroom. I won't charge you rent. You can take some time to find the perfect place of your own."

Flynn smiled hopefully at her.

Her heart fluttered with anticipation. How wonderful would that be? Her gaze trailed over his jaw and up his features. She could totally live with Flynn's sexiness.

Abruptly, her thoughts halted. Wait, no. She couldn't. Being around him constantly would ruin their friendship. Especially now that these weird feelings kept happening.

She forced a smile and said, "Thank you. I have to finish tour and we have studio time booked when it's done so I'll let you know when I get a chance to slow down. It's all in the air right now."

Flynn nodded. He tried to hide it, but she could see the disappointment on his face. He knew that was a no. Flynn said, "Take your time. Finish tour. Do what you gotta do. Standing offer."

She reached across the table and took his hand. "Thank you. I appreciate it."

He clasped her fingers with his. "You're welcome."

Their gazes met right as a shriek rang through the diner. "Oh my God, Flynn's here!"

Flynn frowned. "Shit. Fans," he muttered. "I'm too buzzed for fans."

Flynn let go of Polly's hand and pulled out his wallet. He tucked some bills, more than enough to cover their food and tip, under his half-eaten plate. Flynn shoved his wallet back into his pocket and stood. He reached a hand out to Polly.

She grabbed his hand and quickly they stumbled out a side door, away from where the small group of fans waited at the front of the restaurant.

* * *

Polly and Flynn both giggled as they pushed through the hotel room door.

They entered the room and shut the door. They each fumbled toward the beds, and Polly fell into hers first.

Instead of climbing into his own bed, Flynn climbed into Polly's bed behind her.

"Sweet dreams, Polly."

"Sweet dreams, Flynn."

He wrapped his arms around her, pulled her against him, and they fell asleep wrapped in each other.

Chapter 7
Flynn

Flynn's head throbbed. Expecting to wake up alone, he groaned and stretched. He smacked someone and quickly realized there was a human-shaped ball of warmth in bed beside him.

His eyes flew open. There was definitely a woman in his bed. Shit. Was she a groupie? How drunk had he been? Had he used a condom? Would there be press?

His head pounded, but he tried to focus and glanced at the figure beside him.

Polly. He'd spent the night with Polly. No sex. He breathed a sigh of relief as the memories poured back. He hadn't gotten drunk and slept with a groupie, after all. Flynn had done that when the band first started and thought he'd moved past it.

Warmth filled his chest and made him smile as he watched Polly sleep. She looked so peaceful. He tugged her closer and snuggled his face into her hair. The hotel's rosemary mint shampoo tickled his senses. He inched his nose down further and pressed it to her neck. Mmm. Vanilla and something distinctly Polly. He inhaled deeply.

She stirred and murmured. Flynn pressed her body to his and quietly sang to her. Her warmth comforted him and dulled the throbbing in his head. Quickly, they both drifted back to sleep.

* * *

Polly's cell phone rang, waking her and Flynn. Drowsily, Polly fumbled for her purse, which had fallen off the bed. She pulled the phone out and looked at the screen.

"Unknown caller," she said. She declined the call and tossed the phone on the bedside table.

"What time is it?" Flynn asked.

"1:24."

Flynn rubbed his face and sat up, hanging his legs over the bed. His head throbbed, and he definitely had cotton-mouth.

"We need alcohol," he rasped. "My head is killing me."

"Ugh, mine too. I'm all for some hair of the dog."

"I wonder what room service offers."

Flynn stood and shuffled to the closet, where he riffled through his duffle bag. He found his glasses and pushed them on, then he crossed to the phone at the bedside table which sat between the beds. He picked up the room service menu from beside the phone and thumbed through it.

Flynn said, "Cool, you can order anything from the hotel bar, plus they have an in-house kitchen for meals. I'm going to order drinks and lunch. Any requests?"

Polly shook her head no.

"Hmmm."

Soon, he'd ordered a bottle of rum, plus Polly's favorite meal for lunch: cheeseburgers and fries.

Flynn deposited his glasses onto the bedside table and crossed the room. He pulled a couple of small bottles of alcohol from the mini fridge, then returned to Polly. He climbed into bed with her and handed her a bottle of whiskey. Flynn had tamped down yesterday's jealousy, but he would definitely need some of that alcohol. He opened his bottle.

She opened her bottle and tapped it with his.

"Cheers," she said before downing the bottle whole. Flynn did, too.

They both laid back and rested in silence, waiting for the effects of the alcohol to dull the throbbing in their heads.

"Who called?" Flynn asked after a few minutes.

"Oh, I don't know. It was an unknown number." Polly checked her phone. "They left a voicemail."

Polly pressed her phone to her ear and listened, a frown forming on her lips.

Flynn didn't like it.

"Who was it?" he asked.

She finished listening, then handed the phone to Flynn.

He played the voicemail and listened.

Hey Polly, this is Grady. Listen, I know we didn't end things well and I'm so sorry. I can explain. She and I aren't together anymore. We shouldn't have been in the first place. I let you down. I made a mistake. I'll make it up to you. You're the only one for me. Please call me back.

What a manipulative asshole.

Flynn handed the phone back to Polly and observed her carefully.

"How do you feel about this?" he asked.

She shook her head. "I don't like it."

"Me either. Do you want to hear him out?"

"I... No. He basically said his kids are a mistake and admitted that he cheated on me. And the other stuff I found out... He quit his job, but is pretending he still works there. To top it off, he's got our house for sale."

Flynn flinched. "Seriously? I didn't know the job thing, but I can't believe he thought he could get away with any of it."

Polly shook her head. "I don't understand where we went wrong. I know I was away a lot, but he always said that was fine and the distance now would help establish our future together later. He said it didn't bother him." Tears filled her eyes and one rolled down her cheek.

Flynn turned onto his side, pulled her to him, and hugged her. She wrapped her arms around him, too. Flynn couldn't help but notice that she fit perfectly against him.

He said, "He wasn't right for you. A musician's life is rough. We have to leave behind our homes and the people we love to pursue our music. There's so much travel and distance. But remember, you were just as alone as he was. He chose to cheat. Grady should have talked to you about it, maybe come on tour with you or flew out on a few weekends, not gone behind your back to find someone else. There are ways to cope." He paused, then said, "Honestly, the distance is why Anika broke up with me."

Flynn and Polly hadn't been friends when Flynn and his ex Anika broke up, so Polly didn't know the real story; she would only know what the news reported.

Polly wiped her face and looked at him. "I thought you broke up with her."

"No. That's what she told people. She needed to look innocent for her career, so she lied. The lie's what made the news. That lie helped build my bad boy reputation and I think it helped the band. But it's not what happened. Anika couldn't deal with the distance and ended things."

"Did you love her?"

Flynn paused. "I thought I did. I'm not so sure now. It doesn't matter. My point is, the distance gets in the way sometimes. It's challenging. Not everyone can handle it."

Polly nodded and squeezed him. "I'm sorry she did that to you."

"Thank you. It happened a long time ago and was probably for the best. It doesn't bother me anymore. Are you going to give Grady another chance?" he asked.

"No. It's not like he only cheated. He created a whole family behind my back. And now he wants to walk away from them. It's over. Cheating is bad enough. He did worse. I would always doubt if he was faithful and wonder if he would walk away from our family, too. I can't do it. There was a line he might have come back from, but it's too late. He went way past the line."

He looked at her with pity. "I'm sorry he did this to you."

"I'm glad I found out before we got married... or tried to. That would've been a mess." She laughed dryly.

"You know none of this is your fault, right? It's all on him."

"I know. It doesn't feel like that right now, but I know."

She shifted, and her body rubbed against his. He drew a sharp breath and tried to ignore the friction. His new attraction to her struggled to bloom, but he would try to contain it as best as he could. Polly's hurt was too fresh. The last thing she needed right now was his hard on pushing against her.

She wiped away her tears. The tears broke his heart. He wanted to beat the crap out of Grady.

Flynn said, "You don't deserve to be treated like this. You deserve someone who treats you like a princess. Someone who will give you the world." He kissed her cheek.

"Thank you." She hugged him tight.

"Anytime." He hugged her back.

Someone knocked at the door.

"I'll be right back," Flynn said. He pressed another kiss to Polly's cheek and climbed out of bed.

He grabbed a cash tip from his wallet and crossed the room. He peeked through the peephole and a young man stood outside the door with a bag containing their room service. Flynn opened the door and flashed a smile.

"Thanks, man." He slipped the tip to the guy with a handshake and took the bag.

The man's eyes grew wide. "Y-you're welcome," he stuttered.

Flynn winked and closed the door.

He went back to the bed and sat down beside Polly. He grabbed the rum from the bag, undid the cap, and handed the bottle to Polly.

"Drink up," he said.

"What are we doing later? I don't want to be drunk."

Flynn thought about his plans and laughed. "You'll have more fun if you're tipsy. Trust me."

Polly laughed. "Okay, I'll take your word for it." Polly took a swig of rum straight from the bottle and made a face. "That burns."

Flynn pulled their containers from the bag and handed Polly hers. He piled the ketchup packets on the bed between them and sat against the headboard with his food. Spotting the remote on the bedside table, he grabbed it and turned on a random TV show.

They chowed down on their burgers and fries, as they shared the bottle of rum and laughed at the sitcom.

Tipsy when they were finished, they each changed their clothes in the bathroom then met back at the beds.

"Bring your camera," Flynn said, which Polly obliged.

They stumbled from the hotel into an Uber, luckily without running into fans.

The driver dropped them off on a popular street filled with shops and restaurants. They joined the foot traffic walking up the street before finally sitting on a bench outside of one of the shops.

"What are we doing?" Polly asked.

"Playing tourists. Watch for celebrities and take their pictures."

"But they probably aren't celebrities. I'm tipsy and I can't tell," she protested.

"That's the point. See, look. Doesn't he look familiar? I'm sure I've seen him on TV."

The guy was obviously a random tourist. Polly decided to let it go and have fun instead.

The two had a blast, tipsily making up ridiculous stories and taking pictures of the people they thought looked famous.

At one point, Polly said, "Is that Jason Momoa?" She gasped and snapped a photo.

"I'd bet it is. Damn this street is hopping." Flynn laughed.

A handsome young man approached Polly with a smile. "I saw you from across the street and your beauty struck me. I had to take a chance. Would you be interested in a date?"

Polly opened her mouth to respond, but Flynn's jealousy flared and he growled. "Get lost, pal."

The young man held up his hands and backed away.

"Sorry, I had to ask."

Flynn's gaze settled on Polly, who gave him a weird look and shook her head.

The moment broke when someone shrieked, "Oh my god! Is that Polly? She's with Flynn! Polynn!"

Flynn's face dropped. "And there's our cue to leave," Flynn said. He grabbed Polly's hand and pulled her into the crowd of foot traffic. They disappeared around the corner, losing the fan.

They leaned against a random building, laughing.

"Polynn really caught on, huh?" Polly teased. "You know I'm first because I'm the best, right?"

"I'm not even going there," Flynn laughed. "I admit nothing."

"Aww, come on, you can say it. I rock."

"You do rock. But I refuse to acknowledge this Polynn thing. It's dumb. I won't answer to it."

A crazy thought crossed Flynn's mind and his heart beat a little faster. These combined celebrity names were for couples. Could he and Polly make it as a couple? Would she want to try?

"What, so you'd prefer Flolly?" Polly asked.

Flynn laughed. "Yes actually. Hell of a lot better than 'pollen.' But they only give these combined names to couples."

Flynn had the perfect opportunity and didn't want to miss it. Polly's heartbreak was still fresh, but Flynn's desires were driving him crazy and he needed to take the chance.

He swallowed hard, then asked, "Do you want to be Flolly — a couple — with me?"

"I..." Polly stopped and stared at him. "Are you serious?"

He'd never felt more serious. "I know it's fast, but yeah I am. I want to try if you're willing."

"I'm right out of a long-term relationship," she said.

Flynn took her hand.

"I know," he said. "My timing sucks. But we get along great and I can see a future with you. Plus, I'm going crazy jealous anytime another guy talks to you -- because I want you as mine. If you're up for it, I'd love to try."

Polly stared at him for a moment. His stomach filled with butterflies as he waited for her answer.

"What about the distance?" she asked.

"We can do it." He squeezed her hand. "We'll figure it out. I know we will."

She stared at him for a moment longer, then nodded. "Okay, yes," she said.

Relief flooded him. Flynn grinned. "Yes?"

Polly nodded. "Yes."

"Perfect," he said.

His lips found Polly's. He slid his hands into her hair and ravished her mouth, holding nothing back for their first kiss. Her soft lips matched his and Flynn growled with pleasure.

Conscious that they were still on the street, he reluctantly broke the kiss before they attracted attention.

He smiled at her and said, "Hi," short of breath.

She smiled back. "Hi."

He wrapped her in a hug. "You won't regret this, I promise." He kissed her forehead. He loved the feeling of her in his arms. Why hadn't they done this sooner?

"Thank you," she said.

"For what?"

"That was my only kiss other than Grady. And it blows anything he did out of the water. Thank you for the new memory."

Flynn chuckled and held her close. "We'll make a lot more memories together, don't worry. I fully intend to make that guy a distant past for you. Want to go on our first date? As boyfriend and girlfriend?"

"Sure, what do you have in mind?"

He tipped his head toward a building on the next block. "There's a bowling alley over there."

"Huh. That's a pretty normal first date."

"I know, normal is exotic, right? We never get normal anymore. This'll be a rare treat."

Polly laughed. "Okay, let's do it."

Chapter 8
Flynn

Polly and Flynn clasped hands and walked to the bowling alley. The outside of the building looked old and tired. A bulb flickered in the sign outside.

Inside the front door, it was like they'd stepped back into the 80s. The patterns, colors, and dim bowling floor with flashing lights all seemed retro. Classic rock played over the speakers. A few people bowled, and it looked like a party gathered in a side room, but the place seemed mostly empty.

They checked in at the front desk and got shoes and a lane. Rather than listing their names on the electronic scorecards that showed on the TVs suspended over each lane, Flynn simply entered "Him" and "Her."

Polly turned out to be a master bowler, bowling strike after strike on her turns.

"I used to be in a league," she admitted shyly.

"That's awesome. Did you have a uniform?" Flynn teasingly wiggled his eyebrows at her.

Polly cracked up laughing, then turned to bowl her next set.

Flynn grinned and sang along to the Bon Jovi song playing on the loudspeaker as he waited for Polly to take her turn. Another strike.

A teen approached Flynn hesitantly. Flynn figured he was maybe 15. The kid had black hair, a lip ring, and wore a t-shirt and jeans.

"H - hey, sir," he said.

"Hey, what's up?" Flynn replied.

"I'm sorry to bother you. Are you Flynn from Late Nyght Smoke?"

"Maybe. If I am, I have to swear you to secrecy."

The boy laughed nervously. "The thing is, my sister—" he gestured to the private party room, "—is such a big fan. Today is her 17th birthday. It would really make her day to meet you."

Polly approached and looked between Flynn and the teen curiously.

The boy's eyes grew wide. "You're Polly from Lovely Oblivion."

"Maybe. If I am, promise you won't tell."

Flynn barked a laugh. He loved that they'd reacted the same way.

Flynn waved off Polly's questioning look and said, "I'll tell you later." He turned back to the kid. "What's your name?"

"Josh."

"Josh. If we drop into her party, will she be all right or will she be upset that it's supposed to be 'her' day?"

"She'd love it. There wouldn't be any problem."

Flynn looked at Polly. "What do you say? Want to crash a birthday party?"

Polly smiled. "Sure."

"All right, let's do this. Lead the way," Flynn said.

They followed Josh through the side door to the party room, which had closed after the attendees arrived.

The room was fairly wide and ran the entire length of the bowling alley, it seemed. A small stage sat at one end with a dance floor in front of it, couches and soft chairs throughout the room lent the feeling of comfort. Tables and folding chairs lined the middle, and a pool table sat at the back. A band, which looked to be comprised of teens, played onstage. Party attendees milled around, drinking from solo cups and listening to the music.

Josh led them across the room to a curly haired blond, whose makeup looked perfect and was dressed to kill in a sharp blouse and jeans.

"Ann," Josh said, "I found some special guests to say hello for your birthday."

The girl, Ann, gasped and threw her arms around Flynn. He laughed, patted her back, and quickly extracted himself from her grasp.

"Hi Ann. I'm Flynn. It's nice to meet you."

"I've been your biggest fan for years! I love Late Nyght Smoke," she said.

He smiled. "Thank you. Happy birthday, by the way. This setup is sweet." He gestured to the room, then he put a hand on Polly's back and pulled her closer to him. "This is Polly."

"Oh my god, I know," Ann gushed. "I have all your albums and have attended three of your shows."

Polly grinned. "Thanks. I'm glad you enjoy the music."

"It's so cool to meet you. Hey! Will you play something for us? It would be so amazing." Ann's eyes were wide; her face hopeful.

Flynn looked at Polly, who shrugged.

It would be exciting for these people and they had the time, so why not?

"Sure, we'll play something for the birthday girl," Flynn said, giving Ann his signature grin.

The band was finishing their song. When they finished, Ann rushed onto the stage and interrupted them before they could begin another. She talked to the band for a minute, who seemed agreeable to whatever she said. Their guitarist took off his guitar, leaned it against the wall, and disappeared offstage.

Ann approached the microphone.

"We have some very special guests here today. You may recognize these guitarists, Flynn from Late Nyght Smoke and Polly from Lovely Oblivion. They've agreed to play a birthday song for me. This is such an enormous honor."

Flynn and Polly climbed onto the stage. The guitarist came running back with a second electric guitar, which he plugged into an amp. He passed both guitars off to Flynn and Polly, letting them know the instruments should already be tuned.

They each played a few riffs to warm up, then approached the sole microphone and stood side by side.

The guests crowded around the stage like a mosh pit. Flynn cleared his throat and spoke into the mike. "This'll be rough. We haven't practiced, and neither of us are singers. But we'll give it a shot."

The electric guitars hummed under their fingers. They played a rendition of Happy Birthday, with both of them singing the lyrics. Then they showed off their guitar skills by playing "Dear God" by Avenged Sevenfold. They took turns singing the lyrics and their guitars harmonized together, almost as though they'd practiced a million times.

Flynn grinned. Each stroke of the strings strummed his heart. He felt a tremendous sense of pride watching Polly play, and he loved the flushed glow of her face.

When they finished, the audience went wild. They thanked the crowd, handed the guitars back to their owner, and stepped off stage.

They walked back to Ann, who they gave hugs and wished happy birthday. She offered them food, but they graciously turned it down. Then they high-fived Josh and exited quickly, an effort to avoid a mob. They changed their shoes and dropped their rentals off at the counter, then left the bowling alley.

Flynn and Polly clasped hands and walked along the sidewalk.

"Not bad for a first date, Master Flynn," Polly said. "Oooh look, there's an ice cream shop over there. We should stop for ice cream." Polly pointed at the whimsically decorated shop down the block that reminded Flynn of a fantasy-themed witch's shop.

"We should, huh?" Flynn smiled and ran his tongue over his lips.

"Yes. I want something unique. Like raspberry."

"Well, okay then. Let's see if they have raspberry."

He pressed his hand to the small of her back, and they walked to the shop together.

A bell jingled above the door as they pushed it open and stepped inside.

"Hello," the employee called out. "Come on in. What can I get you?"

A few people sat at the restaurant's tables, but no one noticed them.

They approached the counter and the smiling attendant.

"Hello," Flynn said, wrapping an arm around Polly's shoulder. "The lady will have a double raspberry cone. I'll have a double moose tracks."

"Coming up." The attendant took their money, then started on their cones. When they were ready, Polly and Flynn sat at a table away from the windows to enjoy them.

The alcohol having worn off, they flipped back through their "celebrity" pictures. Most of them were slightly look-alike average people but one photo...

"Holy shit. That was Jason Momoa." Polly laughed and showed Flynn.

"Damn, it was. Nice sighting."

They laughed and ate their ice cream. They traded stories, told jokes, and generally enjoyed their time together.

Chapter 9
Polly

Later, Polly and Flynn snuggled on the hotel bed as they watched a movie together.

Polly's phone chimed. A google alert on her name. When she checked it, a video of her and Flynn playing together popped up on the screen. They looked great, singing and playing guitars together. She wasn't even mad that someone leaked a video when it looked so nice.

Flynn kissed her temple. "Miguel will kill me, but you and I could form our own band if we wanted. We're that good."

Polly laughed and tossed her phone on the bed stand. "Definitely an option."

"What do you want to do about the press?" he asked.

"You mean about us being together?"

"Yeah. The media is going to swarm once we make an announcement. Myself, I don't care. I want to shout from the rooftops that we're together. But I understand if you want to keep things under wraps until the Grady mess blows over."

Polly hugged him. "How about we don't keep it a secret but we don't make an announcement either? Like we tell the people we care about but not the public for now? Not forever, but for a little while."

"That's okay with me."

"Thank you." Polly leaned her forehead against his and drew a breath to speak but then she changed her mind and let it go.

"What is it?" Flynn brushed her hair away from her face.

"I didn't say anything."

"You started to. Tell me what's on your mind."

"I—" She hesitated but Flynn slid his hand to her hip and squeezed to encourage her. "I'm scared, Flynn." She watched concern cross his face.

"Let's talk about it. What are you worried about?"

"It's silly."

"No, it's not. You feel it, which means it's important. Talk to me."

"I don't know. I guess... Well, I guess I'm scared to start another relationship after Grady and I broke up. What if the same thing happens?"

"I would never do that to you."

"But what if you get bored with me or I'm not experienced enough for you?"

She expected Flynn to laugh but instead he took her seriously.

He said, "I will never get bored with you and I don't care about your experience. One, you're amazing and haven't bored me in all the years we've been friends. I will never grow bored with you. Two, I like that you don't have a lot of experience. It means we get to explore new things together and learn what we both like as partners. I find it to be a plus. I swear I won't be unfaithful to you. We have to be open with each other."

"Doesn't the distance concern you?"

Flynn smiled. "No. It's annoying but it's temporary. We'll get past it." His smile faded. He looked at her earnestly. "If you want to try. Will you try with me?"

Talking about her concerns with him lifted a weight off her chest. She wanted to try. Polly nodded. "I'll try with you."

"Thank you."

Flynn nuzzled his nose against her neck and kissed it.

Polly moaned as he licked and kissed her neck gently, with all the patience in the world.

He worked up to her mouth, where he kissed and sucked on her lips.

He rubbed his nose against hers in Eskimo kisses and brushed her hair away from her face.

"I want to do all kinds of naughty stuff with you," Flynn said, twisting her hair around his finger. "I want nothing more than to make love to you right now and claim you as mine. But I understand if you aren't ready for that. It's okay. How do you feel?"

Polly swallowed hard. Flynn was right. She'd ended a lengthy relationship and wasn't sure about sex yet. What if she wasn't good at it and that was why Grady moved on?

"I'd like to wait before we go all the way," she said.

"Okay. Whatever you want. Whenever you're ready." Flynn's lips brushed hers and she melted into him. They laid on their sides and made out like teenagers, their hands roamed and caressed and squeezed as they enjoyed each other. He kissed her throat and left little love bites on her collarbone. They made each other feel good for what seemed like forever, content to be together in their own world.

* * *

Flynn's alarm woke them, tangled together, at 10:30 the next morning. They had to check out by 11:00 and he had to be on his tour bus by 11:30.

"Good morning," Flynn said. He peppered kisses over Polly's face.

"Good morning," she said. She caught his lips with hers, and they both groaned as it morphed into a deep kiss.

Flynn threaded his fingers into her hair and kissed her passionately. His tongue met hers and they almost lost themselves in the kiss.

Polly broke it and nudged Flynn. "We have to get up."

He buried his face in her neck and murmured, "Let's stay here another day. I'll hop on a plane."

"I would love to, but my only flight out is today. I have to catch it. It makes more sense for you to take the bus."

"Not if I buy a plane and fly you myself later. That gets us like 20 more hours together."

Polly laughed. "That's a waste of money and you know it. Plus, you'd have to track a plane down, negotiate, and buy it. That would take away from our time together."

"Still, there's like 18 hours that I didn't have before. Plus, I would ask someone at the label to do it for me so that's a moot argument. It's not like I don't have the money to use. I want to spend the rest of the day with you." He pressed his nose to hers and looked her in the eyes.

"I want to spend the day with you, too." She kissed the side of his mouth. "But I can't let you do that. We have to get up. We can call and video chat all the time. Then we'll be together soon in Boston. Once these tours are done, we can work on being together more."

Flynn growled. "Okay." He climbed out of the bed but turned back to say, "Seriously, think about moving in with me. I don't expect an answer now, but once our tours are over, you do have somewhere to go. Okay?"

"Okay."

Flynn grinned. "I can't wait to live with you."

Polly laughed. "I didn't say yes yet."

"You will."

Flynn winked at her, then disappeared to the bathroom.

* * *

Polly stared at the cloth-lined ceiling of her bunk as she tried to fall asleep that night. The bus was parked outside the venue in Richmond where they would perform tomorrow. Only a few hours had passed, but already she missed Flynn. She was tempted to brew coffee despite the late hour simply to get a whiff of his scent and pretend for a minute that he was nearby instead of a continent away.

Her phone lit up with an incoming call, and Flynn's contact picture flashed across the screen.

"Hello," she answered.

"Hey, how was your flight?" Flynn's low voice murmured.

"Good. How was your drive to the bus?"

"Fine. Uneventful." He paused for a moment. "So what are you wearing?" he teased.

They laughed.

"I'm kidding. Tell me anything you want," he said. "I need to hear you. I already miss you."

"Well on my flight today one of the other passengers..."

The two talked, joked, and told each other stories for hours before Flynn finally said, "I'd better let you get some sleep. I'll talk to you tomorrow night after the show. Are you attending your after party?"

"No."

"Me neither. I'll call you instead."

Those words made Polly's heart soar. Flynn was choosing to spend his time with her instead of at a party with other women.

TABLOID NEWS
"Polynn"

You heard it here first. Late Nyght Smoke guitarist Flynn Morgan and Lovely Oblivion guitarist Polly Worthington are speculated to be Hollywood's newest item! The news comes as a shock, as Flynn hasn't dated since his last disaster with America's Sweetheart, top model Anika Evans, and Polly recently ended her relationship with long-term boyfriend Grady McClelland. The new couple hasn't officially appeared together in public yet but you get the whispers first. Polynn is on shaky ground and who knows if they will make it. A viral video of the two guitarists performing at a birthday party is making waves.

TABLOID NEWS
"Flolly"

Correction. This column previously printed that the potential couple formed by Late Nyght Smoke guitarist Flynn Morgan and Lovely Oblivion guitarist Polly Worthington should be dubbed "Polynn." The speculative couple's nickname is corrected to "Flolly." Stay tuned for more exclusive news about the pair, whose potential relationship is going strong according to this reporter's trusted source.

Chapter 10
Flynn

Late Nyght Smoke positioned themselves on the marked places behind the curtain with their instruments.

"Two minutes and we'll raise the curtain. You guys do your bit, the audience will applaud, and we'll lower the curtain," the TV show's red haired male employee said then checked something on a clipboard.

The band waited on the set of the Late Night Show with Bixby Barnes to perform live. The record label thought the performance would be good marketing.

The employee gave them a get ready signal and disappeared from view. "And now a question from our mailbox," they heard Bixby announce. "This reader says, 'I love Late Nyght Smoke and I would love to hear them perform the Chip 'N Dale Rescue Rangers theme song. Thank you. Veronica N.' You heard it, folks. In honor of this reader's letter, tonight we have Late Nyght Smoke in the house performing the Rescue Rangers theme song!"

The curtain raised and lights shined onto the band. The audience screamed as they launched into the music.

Flynn enjoyed the whimsy of the song and his fingers flew over his guitar while Will belted the lyrics.

"Yeah!" Will shouted as they finished and they all bowed.

"Ladies and gentlemen, that was Late Nyght Smoke performing the Rescue Rangers theme song. Fantastic!" Bixby announced as the curtains closed. "Veronica, thanks for the request!"

Flynn removed his guitar strap from his shoulders and leaned his guitar against the drums. The show's employees quickly moved the band offstage and into a dressing room. Stylists and makeup artists went to work to make them camera-ready for their upcoming interview.

Flynn sat back in the makeup chair and let them do their work in silence. He missed Polly. He wanted to see her soon but he wasn't sure when because of both their jobs. What could he do in the meantime? Flowers? Presents? What would make her smile?

He thumbed through his phone browser as he thought about it, and finally decided to use a florist. With a grin, he ordered a dozen roses, a bottle of Polly's favorite wine, and a box of chocolates for delivery to her at Lovely Oblivion's next venue. The card was to read: *Polly, Thinking of you. Talk soon. With love, Flynn*

He hoped she liked the gifts.

Someone knocked at the dressing room door and poked their head in. The redheaded employee from earlier appeared. "Five minutes. Hurry it up." The door closed as quickly as it had opened and the artists rushed to put the final touches on everyone.

They all dressed in business casual outfits complete with ties. Flynn felt stuffy and adjusted his tie. He rolled the sleeves of his green shirt up to his elbows, which revealed his tattoos. He shrugged his shoulders and smiled at the stylist that glared at him.

The band was ushered from the room to line up beside the Late Show's set. Three small sofas sat mid-stage in a semicircle and the host's desk sat on the far side of the sofas.

"And now please welcome Late Nyght Smoke," Bixby said.

The guys grinned and waved at the audience as they walked onstage to the sofas. They all settled in and their host, a thin middle aged man with silver hair named Bixby, sat on the middle sofa beside Will.

"This is awesome. It's great having you guys here," Bixby said. "Thanks for agreeing to appear on the show."

"Sure thing," Will said with a smile. "We're big fans. Thanks for asking us."

"What have you guys been up to?"

"We're working on new songs, finishing our tour, and we have studio time booked this spring," Will said.

"Does this mean there's a new album soon?"

Will grinned and tucked his blond hair behind his ear. "It does. We've been telling people 'summer' but we have some exciting news for you tonight."

"What's that?"

"Our next album will be released on June 27. You're the first to hear it."

Cheers went up from the crowd.

"How exciting! Congratulations!" Bixby said.

"Thanks," Will said. "We'll be recording next spring and fans can expect more music they'll love. Once we're done recording, we're touring again. Tickets go on sale tomorrow."

"You hear that, folks? Where can fans get more information?"

"Check out the band website and ticketmaster for more info," Zack chimed in.

"That's great news. I'm excited for the new music."

"Thanks," Will said. He smiled.

Bixby looked at Flynn. "People are dying to know, what's going on between you and Polly Worthington?"

Flynn smiled softly. "I'd love to tell you, Bixby, but that's between me and Polly. We've known each other for years, and she is a wonderful person. That's all I'll say."

"That's disappointing. Are you sure you won't give us the scoop on Polynn?"

"Flolly," Flynm corrected without thinking. He offered Bixby a sheepish grin. "If Polly and I would happen to date, we'd prefer Flolly."

"Is anything going on there?"

"Sorry, no comment." Flynn flashed an apologetic smile at Bixby.

The host moved on to other topics and the band enjoyed a lively show with him. Flynn had fun but he only half paid attention, his thoughts on Polly.

TABLOID NEWS
"Flolly Update"

While no announcement has occurred, Late Nyght Smoke guitarist Flynn Morgan hinted at a relationship between himself and Lovely Oblivion guitarist Polly Worthington on last night's Late Night Show with Bixby Barnes. Morgan confirmed that should the couple ever need a nickname, they want to use Flolly. Let this column be the first to call it. If they are not currently dating, Flolly will become a reality soon. Watch for more updates here.

Chapter 11
Polly

"Ms. Worthington, here is your room key," the female hotel desk clerk said and slid a key card across the counter to Polly. "Also, there was a delivery for you. We left it in your room. Thank you for your stay at the Felton Inn." She smiled.

A delivery? What would that be?

"Thank you." Polly returned the smile, picked up the key, and went to the elevator. She rode it to the third floor, walked down the hallway to her room, and let herself in.

A vase of gorgeous roses sat on the room's table. A bottle of wine and a box of chocolates sat by them.

"Oh," she breathed. She tossed her duffle bag on the floor and crossed the room to the table. She grinned when she realized it was her favorite wine. This had to be from Flynn.

She plucked the card from its holder in the flowers and opened it. *Polly, Thinking of you. Talk soon. With love, Flynn*

How sweet. Grady never did anything like this for her. Warmth flooded her chest as she considered the thoughtful gesture.

She put the card on the table and picked up the wine and chocolates. She crossed the room and climbed under the soft, fluffy comforter. Polly picked up the remote and turned on a random movie.

She settled onto the pillows and opened the wine and chocolates. A moan escaped her lips when she took the first bite of decadent chocolate. Delicious.

Polly pulled her phone out to text Flynn.

Polly: Thank you for the gifts
Flynn: YW. Enjoy. Wsh i cld do more
Polly: They are perfect. Thank you.
Flynn: Did thy mke u smile?
Polly: Definitely
Flynn: Goal accmplishd

Polly snapped a sultry selfie of herself biting into a chocolate and texted it to Flynn.

Flynn: Gorgeous
Polly: TY
Flynn: Tht's going in my spank bank
Polly: LOL
Flynn: Wht? I cn imgn thse lips arnd my cock. Gvg a lttl suck... Tht pic wll hlp
Polly: It's early and I'm sure you have somewhere to be so I won't start down the sext rabbit hole with you right now. What are your plans for today?
Flynn: Ugh. I do. Mtng w label ltr thn show. Cn cll u aftr
Polly: I can't wait. :)
Flynn: Me ethr. I miss u
Polly: I miss you too
Flynn: I'll chk the schdl 2 c whn I'm off & cn c u nxt
Polly: Me too. I'd love to see you on your next break
Flynn: We'll set smthg up. Soon. I prmse
Polly: Soon. Have a nice day
Flynn: Thx. U 2

Polly settled in to watch the movie. She drank straight from the bottle of wine, ate her chocolates, and relaxed in her hotel bed. She flipped through the channels and found a movie she'd seen a thousand times. She watched TV, drank wine, ate chocolate, and settled in. Flynn's gifts put the final perfect touch on her day off.

Chapter 12
Flynn

Late Nyght Smoke and their manager gathered around the conference room table and waited for the record label executives to show up.

"I understand the high-ups want to try a new sound to bring in new fans. Try to be receptive to what they say," Miguel said.

"Why?" Will, their lead singer, asked. "We're doing fine."

"You can never have enough fans. Try to be open to their suggestions," Miguel said.

The door opened and two people walked in, a sharply dressed man and woman. They took seats at the end of the table.

The man smiled. "Hi, nice to meet you all. I'm Brad and this is my associate Jane." The woman waved.

"Sorry to bring you all down here," Brad said. "I won't keep you long. I'd like to discuss a sound change."

"To what?" Flynn asked. He wrote most of the songs and didn't like the sound of this.

"We'd like a few songs with a pop vibe. Peppy. You have a dark sound, which your fans obviously love, but we'd like to add a few more upbeat songs and maybe bring in some new fans."

Flynn growled. "The fans will hate it."

Brad held up his hand in a placating gesture. "Not if you do it right. Just a few songs. Let's say three. We'll bring in one of our top writers to help and make sure you stay true to your roots but meet the sound we're looking for."

"I don't like it. I won't do it," Flynn said.

Jane cleared her throat. "I'm sorry, Mr. Morgan, but you are under contract with this record label and we are telling you to do it. You do what we say. You don't have a choice."

"Excuse me?"

"You heard me." Jane and Brad stood.

"You're going to lose good fans. They'll say we sold out," Flynn protested.

"We're counting on you to write peppy enough songs that it won't matter," Brad said. "You'll replace any fans you lose."

"This is bullshit."

"Give it a try," Brad said. "Consider us the experts." He and Jane walked to the door of the conference room. "Thanks for meeting with us. We appreciate your time." Brad closed the door behind them.

"Fuck," Flynn exploded and banged his fist against the table. "Why didn't you warn us, Miguel?"

"I didn't know. No one said anything to me."

"The fans love our sound. This is a really bad idea," Flynn said.

"I'd say write the songs. If you don't make any progress or don't like them, then we won't release the songs," Miguel said.

"You heard Brad and Jane. They're threatening our contract." Flynn gestured at the door.

"Right now they are. Write the songs. Cooperate. I'll work on them in the meantime. When the release date gets here, if you don't like the songs for the band's image then we won't release them."

"That's not what they said."

"I'll work on them. Trust me."

"If they insist on this, we need to look at getting out of this contract and finding a new label," Flynn said.

"Don't worry. I've got this. Go along with them for now."

* * *

Polly

Polly jammed out while lying down and wiggled in her hotel bed to the music pulsing through her headphones. She moved her feet and arms, and mouthed the catchy song. It was late and the rest of the band was sleeping in their rooms.

She held her camera in front of her face and clicked through the picture viewer at the images on the SD card. The awards show, playing tourists with Flynn, the "celebrities" they'd seen on the street, and goofy pictures of them together at the hotel room. The images each brought a smile to her face.

Polly's phone rang. A quick glance showed Flynn calling. His show must be over.

She pulled her headphones out and answered.

"Hey," she said.

"Hey. How was your day?"

"Good. Yours?"

Flynn sighed. "I've had better, but overall not the worst."

"Oh, I'm sorry. Is there anything I can do to help?"

"Talk to me. Help me keep my mind busy."

"Okay. Do you want to talk about what happened?"

Flynn sighed and made a noise of frustration. "No."

"Okay. What's your third favorite dinosaur?" Polly asked.

Flynn laughed. "Not my first?"

"Nope. Third."

"Random. God, I don't know. I haven't thought about dinosaurs since I was a kid."

"Think about them now."

"Umm. Brachiosaurus. Because I think they look cool but not as cool as my favorite."

"Nice. What's your favorite?"

"Velociraptors. Those things were awesome."

Polly laughed. "Now, if you could have any superpower, what would it be?"

Flynn laughed. "Any superpower, huh?"

"Yep. X-ray vision, invisibility, or whatever you want."

"Hmm."

"No rules."

"Exact-Change Man. I would have the ability to have exact change at any occasion, no matter what. If I needed to buy something, I would reach into my pocket and have the exact amount of the sale, every time. Whether $1 or $1.3 billion dollars."

"You'd better have some big pockets for that billion dollar purchase," Polly laughed.

"Hey, I'll be sure to wear baggy pants. I may need to buy you bookoos of flowers sometime," he teased. "You know what I mean. What about you?"

"I'd want to be incredibly lucky. Have everything work out for the best result and go my way."

"Hmm. That doesn't seem like it would be useful on the surface but that could actually be very useful when it comes down to it."

"I know, right? If you had to pick a song to represent your life, what would you choose?"

"Damn, that's a deep question."

"It is. First thoughts?"

"Right now, my first thought is 'Fuck Her Gently' by Tenacious D."

Polly laughed. "You're bad."

"What, you asked. It's not my fault you're on my mind." Flynn laughed. "What's your pick?"

"Mine is 'High Hopes' by Panic! At The Disco. It's about always shooting for the best and working toward what you want."

"Nice choice. What do I have to do to work toward you moving in with me?"

"Flynn!"

He laughed. "Sorry."

Polly and Flynn talked for hours about anything and everything. She successfully distracted him until they both fell asleep with the call still connected.

Chapter 13
Flynn

Flynn flicked his head backward and flung sweat out of his hair as he walked offstage. He handed his guitar to a nearby roadie, and strode to the dressing room along with the other band members, who chattered loudly, excited about how well the performance went.

Someone had taped a piece of paper to the door that read "Late Nyght Smoke." The band members opened the door and walked through. Flynn followed through last and shut the door behind them.

He did a double take when he spotted a beautiful redhead on the room's couch. She sat beside their manager, Miguel. She and Miguel stood. The woman flipped her hair behind her shoulder, her silver dress hugging her frame.

Miguel said, "Guys, this is your new songwriter, Amie Athey. She has a lot of writing experience, and I think you'll do great together. She will travel with you to write and hopefully spark your next hit."

Their label mentioned possibly bringing on a songwriter for the next album, but this was a surprise. They weren't even having trouble writing, but the label wanted a few songs with a different sound to attempt to hit the pop charts.

The woman approached their lead singer, Will, who looked at her with confusion. "Uhh, hi?" he asked, tucking his blond hair behind his ear.

She held her hand out to shake Will's and smiled. "Hi. I'm Amie. Pleased to meet you."

Will cleared his throat. "Pleased to meet you, too," he said awkwardly. He turned to gesture at Flynn. "Flynn here does most of our writing, so you'll probably be working mainly with him."

Amie shook hands with the other band members, then approached Flynn and shook his. "I'm sure we'll be a great team."

Irritation nagged at Flynn, but he tried to ignore it.

"Sure." Flynn let go of her hand. "Nice to meet you." He glanced at the guys. "I'm going to hit the showers, then head back to the bus and call Polly. I'm not going to the after party."

"Okay, man. Tell her we said hi," Will said.

"Will do."

Flynn headed into the dressing room bathroom and shut the door behind him. He stripped off his clothes, turned on the water, and let the hot stream run over him, washing away some of his irritation.

* * *

"So the label wants some 'peppier' songs to draw in a new crowd. I really think that idea will flop because that's not our band's sound. But they've hired this songwriter, Amie, to try to achieve it. I'm trying not to be annoyed, but I'm very annoyed," Flynn said, holding the phone to his ear as he stretched out in his bunk. The other band members hadn't returned yet, so quiet surrounded him.

"I'm sure it will work out fine. I can always write with you, though I'm not sure they'll be sold on my version of peppy," Polly said, then made a fake upbeat guitar riff sound.

Flynn laughed. He'd seen her that morning, but already missed her.

"Miguel said sales for my band are up after that video of you and me went viral. How about you?"

"Same. My manager, Paige, actually said maybe we should have you do a guest appearance and sing a duet."

"With you?"

"Probably with Bex."

Flynn shook his head no. "Mmm. No. I don't like that."

Polly laughed. "Well fine, you don't have to do a duet with my band if you don't want to."

A smirk stretched across Flynn's face. "Polly."

"What?"

"I don't want to do a duet with Lovely Oblivion."

"Okay, fine. You said that."

"I like Bex, as a friend anyway, but I don't want to sing with her. Won't work. I want to sing a duet with you."

Polly sucked in a breath. "What? Really?"

"Yep. Let's write a song and sing it together. Flynn and Polly. Flolly." He chuckled. "Not Late Nyght Smoke and Lovely Oblivion."

"Yeah, I'd love that. Let's do it.'

Flynn smiled. "Okay."

Polly yawned. "I'm sorry, Flynn. It's like 3:00 am here and I'm worn out."

"That's okay. Get some sleep then. We can talk tomorrow." Flynn wanted to keep her on the phone, but his lady needed her rest.

"Are you sure?"

"Yeah, of course."

"Sweet dreams."

"Sweet dreams."

* * *

Three weeks later

Amie slid onto the cushion beside Flynn on the bus's leather couch. She pressed against his side and put her hand on his guitar frets.

"What about this key?" she asked.

He shifted uncomfortably for a moment, then strummed the acoustic guitar. A solid chord rang out, higher than they normally played.

"I don't know if Will can match that pitch," he said.

"Let's try it. We can always lower it down an octave if we need to."

She let go of the fret but stayed close to Flynn.

"Can you scoot over? I'm a little squished," Flynn said. Having Amie that close made him uncomfortable. She'd been trying to hit on him, and he didn't like it.

"Oh sure, honey."

She scooted away, but only about half an inch.

He cleared his throat with annoyance. "A little more." Scoot. "A little more." Scoot. This time, she was a respectable distance away. "Thank you."

"Oh, sure. I think we have a good start. Two songs written already and knocking this third one out soon."

Flynn nodded. "I am curious what the label thinks. Our songs don't usually sound like this. This is more pop rock than we've ever done," he said, strumming the guitar.

"This could catapult you guys into ultimate stardom. Your music is so dark right now, maybe stepping a foot into pop will be a catalyst."

Flynn shook his head. The band was doing fine and the pop angle was a waste of time. Their fans wouldn't want it. He didn't know that the band wanted new fans who did. He'd told the label that.

"It's nice how optimistic you are," he said. "But I doubt it. We aren't 'peppy.' The fans will not like this."

Will came forward from the bunk area and plopped down beside Amie on the couch. He grabbed a controller and turned on the TV.

"Excuse me, Will," Amie said. "Would you mind keeping the sound low? We're working on a song."

"Sure," Will said.

Flynn scoffed. He wanted to do anything but work with Amie right then.

"Actually," Flynn said and stood, "I don't feel that creative right now. Let's try again later."

"Oh, okay." Amie stood and touched Flynn's arm, concern in her eyes. "Are you feeling all right?"

He shrugged her off, irritated that she touched him.

"I'm tired. I'm going to lie down for a while. No worries. Maybe you and Will can work on a song for now."

Will grinned and placed a hand on the couch beside her. "Let's do that."

"Oh, okay," Amie said.

Flynn left the guitar propped on the couch and walked to his bunk. He climbed in and pulled the curtain shut behind him. With a sigh of irritation, he settled onto his pillow. He took a moment to decompress, then smiled when he saw the photos he'd mounted on the ceiling. Center, he had the photo of Polly and him from the hotel with their clashing clothes. He'd surrounded that with other photographs, memories, from their trip.

He sent Polly a text.

Flynn: Time to talk?

Polly: Sure.

His phone rang, and he answered with a smile. "Hi."

"Hey," Polly said. "How are you?"

"Perfect, now that I'm talking to you."

Polly giggled. "How's the songwriting going?"

"Great. We have two songs done and are working on a third. I still think it's a waste of time."

"It'll work out. Is Amie fitting in okay on a bus full of guys?"

"She's doing fine. We aren't barbarians," he teased.

"I know you aren't. I adore you guys. I would tour with any of you, anytime." Polly cleared her throat and hesitated a second, then she said, "It's not you guys I'm worried about. Amie makes me nervous."

Flynn narrowed his eyes at the bunk's ceiling. "What do you mean?"

"I... Well, I'm a continent away. She's right there on the bus and she's gorgeous. I'm-I'm afraid she'll turn into a warm body to pass the time. I guess I'm... Well, I'm insecure about being so far away and having her right there. She's accessible."

Flynn flinched. "I wouldn't do that to you."

"Logically, I know that. We talked about it already. I'm insecure about it, though. Grady fucked up my trust. It makes no sense and you've given me no reason to worry, but the distance bothers me. I wish I could be there with you."

"I know. I wish you could, too. You'll be with me as soon as we can make it happen. Try not to worry. I want to be with *you*. I need you to trust me. Before we know it, Boston will be here and we can have some time together."

"I do trust you. But Grady gave me all this insecurity. I'll work on it. I'm sorry."

He hated that she'd been through that. "Nah, don't be sorry. Work through it with me. Talk to me. If you're worried about anything, talk to me. Be confident that I won't hurt you."

"Okay."

"I'm purely professional with Amie. She's only here until the label tells her to leave. I'm completely taken by my girlfriend, who has nothing to worry about."

"Oh really? Who is this girlfriend you mention?"

A smile touched Flynn's lips. "Only the most amazing woman in the world. She's a musician and a photographer, and I absolutely love her."

Polly sucked in a breath. "Do you mean it?"

"I do."

"I love you, too."

Flynn grinned. "Good. Because I'm all yours."

TABLOID NEWS
"Lack of Inspiration"

Late Nyght Smoke reportedly hired a songwriter to assist them, as their inspiration has lacked for months. The news comes after their song "What It Means" obtained Song of the Year recently. With lack of inspiration in the lyric pool, maybe fresh ears will produce another hit song. Lead singer Will said, "We can use all the help we can get." We'll see how well this songwriter helps the band.

Chapter 14
Polly

Polly wrapped the towel around her wet hair and dried it after her shower. She tossed the towel in a hamper, then she slid on old jeans and a tank top. She pulled on tennis shoes and walked from the shower into the dressing room. The post-show excitement had died down and only Greg remained in the room, talking on his phone.

Polly made sure she had her phone and billfold in her pockets, then she left the dressing room and walked down the hallway to the outside door.

She nodded at security by the door and walked outside into the cool night air.

Her feet crunched the gravel across the parking lot to the bus. She fist-bumped their security guard, and he opened the door to the bus stairs.

The rest of the band plus their significant others, Ryker and Aiden, crowded into the front lounge, and watched their lead singer, Bex, kick butt at Mario Kart. She stuck her tongue between her teeth and bit it as she concentrated, her short hair spiked into a mohawk. A "go, go, go" chant started as Polly walked up the aisle to her bunk.

She climbed into her bunk and pulled the closure shut behind her. She checked the time. Flynn would be onstage on the west coast right now.

She went online and searched for the concert. Their band was doing a live stream. Polly bought a ticket and tuned her phone into the performance. Sweat ran off Flynn as he played a guitar riff. He looked hot in his tight t-shirt and jeans. She closed her eyes and listened to Late Nyght Smoke play the concert.

Polly fell asleep to the music. A few hours later, she woke when her phone rang. Flynn. She smiled.

"Hello?" she answered.

"Hey, Polly. How was your day?" His deep voice rumbled in her ear.

"Good. How about yours?"

"Not bad."

"I caught part of your show."

"Oh yeah?"

"You looked smokin' onstage. Apparently, I'm dating a hot rocker."

Flynn laughed. "You certainly are. I'm the hottest."

Polly laughed. "You are. I miss you."

"I miss you, too. Don't worry, we'll be together soon."

"I know. It can't come soon enough. Only a few more shows and we can spend some time together."

A minute passed, and Flynn made a frustrated noise. "I'm sorry. I was thinking about your stage outfit. You always look great. So great, I want to peel that outfit off you. It's all I can think about. I know you need to wait and god knows I'll wait as long as you need, but I want you. I keep thinking about all the things we could do together... I'm sorry. I need a minute and I'll be good."

Polly's breath caught. She knew Flynn was trying to be courteous and wait until she was over her last relationship, but she wanted him terribly... She was ready for intimacy with Flynn.

"Flynn..." she said.

"I'm sorry. Give me a minute." She heard him breathing meditatively.

"Flynn. I'm ready."

"What?"

"If you were here, I'd slide my hand onto your cock over your pants and stroke you."

Flynn's breath hitched. "Polly, don't say it unless you mean it."

"I mean it."

He hesitated, then he asked, "Are you sure?"

"Yes."

"Are you alone?"

She could still hear the party in the front lounge. Everyone would be up there for a while. "Yes."

"What are you wearing?"

"A tank top and jeans."

"Mmm. If I were there, I'd press kisses all over the exposed skin of your neck and down your chest. I'd pull your tank top down and pull your bra down. I'd release those beautiful breasts and swirl my tongue over each of your nipples." He groaned. "I'm hard thinking about what I'd do to you. I'd lick and suck your nipples — wide strokes, soft flicks, rhythmic tugs. I'd worship them and keep at it until you begged me for more."

She closed her eyes and whimpered. His words worked their magic.

"Touch yourself for me," he murmured. "Pull your shirt down and play with your nipples. Make them feel good. Strokes only. Don't squeeze them yet."

With one hand, Polly tugged her shirt and bra down until her breast popped free. She brushed her thumb over a nipple, which immediately hardened from the contact. A small noise escaped her.

"Good," Flynn encouraged. "Keep going. Let me hear you."

She propped the phone beside her head to free her hands. Polly released her other breast from her clothes and stroked that nipple. Both hands came to her chest, and she flicked both hardened nubs. She moaned quietly.

"Beautiful," Flynn murmured.

"You touch yourself for me," she said.

"Oh, I am," he said. "I'm so hard right now and it's all for you." He groaned. "I'm stroking myself slowly, thinking of you. I have pre-come moistening the tip and I'll spread it over my cock, imagining you did it."

She ran her thumbs over her nipples. She brushed and flicked them, teased them until she whimpered.

"Perfect," Flynn said. "Now squeeze your nipples for me. Together."

Polly moaned as her fingers simultaneously pinched her nipples, and pleasure coursed through her body.

"God, yes." Flynn drew an audible deep breath, then breathed a little harder. "Rub your clit. Tell me how wet you are."

Polly reached down and opened her jeans. She slid her fingers between her lips and swirled them around her clit.

"I'm drenched for you," she murmured.

"Good. Get yourself there. I'll do it for you myself next time, but I need you to do it for me now."

She slid her fingers over her clit and pressed harder. Her breathing audibly increased, and she whimpered. Flynn groaned and panted.

"Come for me, beautiful. I'm almost there with you," Flynn said.

His noise and encouragement drove her crazy and pushed her orgasm closer.

She rubbed harder and faster. "Flynn," she moaned softly. "I want you to have your way with me. I want you to come inside me, fill me up."

"Oh fuck yeah, Polly," he grunted and groaned as he reached his release.

His orgasm pushed her over the edge. "Yes," Polly breathed, her orgasm pulsing through her.

They both laid there for a minute, and they panted as they enjoyed the post-orgasm euphoria.

"I can't wait to make you orgasm in person," Flynn murmured. "I bet you're even more gorgeous when you come."

Polly giggled. "Thank you. I'm sure I am," she teased.

Flynn chuckled. "That was the first time I've ever had phone sex, and it was hot. I never come that fast."

"Same. Something about it was really sexy, though. I liked it."

She could hear his smile through the phone. "Me, too."

Polly closed her eyes, fixed her clothes, and rested against the pillow.

Flynn cleared his throat. "Hey, Polly."

"Yeah?" She opened her eyes and stared at the ceiling.

"Are you on birth control? Boston is coming up soon and I want to make sure I have protection if we need it."

She smiled. "Are you clean, Flynn?"

"I am. The label makes us get tested once a year. The last test was clean and I haven't been with anyone since."

"Same. Plus, I'm on the pill. We're good, Flynn."

He groaned. "You mean I get to have you bare?"

"If you want."

"You have no idea how much I want." He laughed. "I love you, Polly."

"I love you, too."

Chapter 15
Flynn

The fans screamed outside the venue and pushed against the barrier walkway between the venue and the bus. Flynn wiped the sweat from his face as his band walked from the venue toward the bus.

"Check out those chicks." Zack nudged Flynn with his elbow and nodded toward a group of four scantily clad female groupies. "I bet any of them would be happy to do whatever we want."

"Feelin' frisky, huh?"

"Always. Come on, man. Enjoy them with me."

Flynn put his hand on Zack's shoulder. "I can't. I won't. They don't do it for me anymore. But that leaves more for you."

"Are you turning into a one-woman man?"

"I think I am. I only have eyes for Polly these days."

"Pussy," Zack laughed. Flynn raised an eyebrow, and Zack held up his hands in surrender. "I'm kidding. Good for you. I'm happy for you. Leaves more for me." Zack slapped him on the back.

Flynn chuckled. "Good luck, Zack. Keep in mind, we only have a few hours before we roll out."

"Plenty of time."

The band stopped to sign autographs and take pictures with the fans, but quickly Flynn was back on the bus and in his bunk, alone. He flipped through the photos on his phone from his trip with Polly and smiled. He missed her. He couldn't wait until they could spend more time together.

* * *

The bus rolled toward their next location and the rest of the band slept, but Flynn was restless. Polly was already asleep, so he couldn't call her. He sat on the couch in the front lounge and played his acoustic guitar. He played his heart out, made up guitar solos, and plucked random songs. At this hour, it was him and his guitar. He loved music and would be content to practice alone all night.

After he'd played for two hours or so, Amie appeared from the bunks, her hair ruffled and pajamas on.

Flynn frowned. Amie liked to hit on him, and he didn't like being alone with her.

She yawned. "Can't sleep?" she asked.

"Nope. Figured I'd get some practice in instead."

She sat down at the table across the aisle from him and watched him.

"Look, I know you don't like me," she said. "Can we simply focus on making music together?"

Flynn stopped playing the guitar and leveled his gaze at her.

He said, "For the record, I don't dislike you. I don't think this music experiment you're conducting will work, but I'm game and I'll try it. I need you to understand, though. I'm not available to date. You want to make music? Fine. Professionally. Personally, no. I don't appreciate the passes you've made at me. Don't hit on me again. Keep your actions professional and we can work together. I'll be civil. But I won't tolerate anything but professional. It's disrespectful to my girlfriend, and I won't put up with that shit."

Her eyes widened. "I'm sorry. I wasn't trying to cross a line."

"Well, you did. Professional only."

"Okay. I'm sorry."

Flynn nodded. "Don't let it happen again."

"I won't."

Flynn leaned back and played the guitar, his fingers plucking across the strings.

"Hey, if you shorten the last two notes, you might have something there," she said.

Flynn replayed the tune.

"Yeah, like that."

They productively worked on new songs for a few hours before Amie went back to bed. Flynn chose to stay up all night and work on his duet for Polly.

He sent her a text before she woke up.

Flynn: Can't sleep. Thinking of you. Writing an epic guitar duet for us. You're going to love it. This could be one of many. Maybe we should start our own band ♥

Soon, Will woke and joined Flynn on the couch. They quickly entered a video game battle that lasted for hours and passed the time until the next stop.

* * *

"We think this will be great PR for both of you," Miguel said. "You don't actually have to date, but show up at a few events together and take pictures with her. Smooch in public occasionally. It'll look great for both your images."

Flynn and Miguel stood outside the bus at Late Nyght Smoke's latest stop.

The record label and the PR team wanted Flynn to "take back" his ex, Anika, for the public eye. They asked for a contract certifying that Flynn and Anika would appear together so often per month and have so many "accidental" kiss pictures per year.

The thought disgusted Flynn and made him want to punch someone.

Miguel said, "Look, I know you recently started dating Polly, but the public doesn't know that. They still think you're only good friends. This would be a huge image boost for you, Anika, and the band."

Flynn shook his head no and said, "No. I'm with Polly. If anything, she and I being together will be an image boost for us. I'm pissed off that we're even having this conversation."

"It will really be good for your image after all the fallout from your break up with Anika. Turn you into more of a family man. The bad boy gets tamed."

Flynn scoffed. "That's not my fault. I told you what happened. Anika broke up with me. You—" Flynn moved his finger in a collective circle that included Miguel, the PR team, and the record label "—decided not to tell the public that little fact and you've been perfectly happy to ride on the coattails of the fall out since. It's not my fault you didn't correct her lies."

"There's also a hefty cash bonus in this if you sign."

"What?" Flynn's anger flared. He punched the side of the bus. While the bus's body didn't dent, he hit it hard enough to bust open his knuckles.

"Flynn, your hands!" Miguel practically panicked.

"Miguel, step the fuck away from me. Now," Flynn gritted.

Miguel held his hands up and slowly backed away.

"Tell the record label, I'm with Polly. I will never date Anika again, even if it's fake. I don't want a fucking cash bonus to pretend to date my ex. And if they come to me about another image boost idea, Polly had better be the other person or they can forget it. I won't cheat on her or look like I cheated on her, even if it's only a pretend image thing."

Miguel gestured with his hands, something that was probably supposed to be calming. "Okay. I'll tell them."

Flynn turned and stalked onto the bus without another word.

He closed the door behind him and stormed up the aisle to the restroom. He grimaced as he ran water over his busted knuckles. The water tinted red as it washed away the blood.

He couldn't bring himself to pretend with Anika, even if Polly would have been okay with it. The thought disgusted him. He was with Polly. Images of him in a relationship with someone else, even for publicity, were a route he would never step down.

Chapter 16
Polly

Polly ran off the tour bus and hurled herself into Flynn's arms. He wrapped his arms around her and hugged her close.

"God, you feel so good." He pressed a kiss to her hair. "And you smell delicious." He drew a deep breath of her hair.

Polly tugged his mouth down to hers and kissed him.

Flynn kissed her back with everything. He picked her up, wrapped her legs around his waist, and rubbed delicious friction against her jeans. She wrapped her arm around his neck and kissed him back.

He broke the kiss and grinned at her. "Hi."

She smiled and squeezed her legs around him. "Hi."

Bex's husband, Aiden, walked by them and whistled. "Damn, guys. Not in public. The venue has storage rooms that work great if you're in a hurry." He wagged his eyebrows as if he knew from experience, then climbed into the bus. Flynn and Polly laughed and separated.

Flynn took her hand and clasped his fingers with hers. "We have to figure out how to be together more often. I miss you when we're apart."

"I know. This tour is almost over. Maybe we can tour together next year or something."

"Man, I hope so. That would rock. I'm making that suggestion to Miguel." Flynn leaned down and pressed a kiss to her cheek. "Well, we made it to Boston. What's your itinerary look like?"

"I've got so much to see with you. What's yours like?"

"Did you plan both days?"

"Of course."

Flynn smiled like he had a secret. "Which day do you perform?"

"Tonight."

"Okay. I play tomorrow. I already checked into the hotel. Let's head over there and we can combine our plans."

"Okay."

They caught a cab from the venue to the hotel, where they stashed Polly's luggage in Flynn's room. It didn't escape her notice that the room had a single king sized bed. She flushed when she thought about how they'd use it later.

They sat at the room's table and pulled out their phones. They loaded their itinerary lists and switched phones.

Surprisingly, she didn't recognize any of the locations on Flynn's list.

She said, "There's only one day on your list. And I don't think any of these locations are in Boston."

Flynn smirked. "Correct." He handed her phone back.

"So where are they?"

"You planned two days, right? Which day do you look forward to the most?" he asked.

"Umm. Day two, I guess."

He smiled. "Okay, so I have a compromise for you. I know you said to plan two days and we would merge them, but I didn't do that. I only planned one."

"I see that."

"Let's do one day of yours and one day of mine. We'll do whichever day you're most excited about then my day. Or if you want to combine yours into a new list, that's fine, too."

Polly slid his phone across the table to him. "Where are the locations on your list exactly?"

"Not far, don't worry."

Polly pursed her lips. "Okay, fine. But I can't miss the show."

"You won't. Don't worry."

"My list first?" she asked.

"Sure."

"I hope you're ready for a full day. We have a lot to cover."

Flynn smiled. He crossed to his luggage, pulled on a ball cap, and tossed one to her. "Lead the way."

Polly and Flynn spent a beautiful fall day touring Boston. They visited the Boston Public Library, the Paul Revere House, and the New England Aquarium, where Polly got a great picture of Flynn posing in front of the sea turtles. They stopped for ice cream before they left the aquarium. Soon, they headed to the Visitors Information Center, where they joined the Freedom Trail walking tour led by a guide dressed as a colonial, who showed them many of the attractions from Boston Common to Faneuil Hall. They had a wonderful day out, where they laughed, chatted, and enjoyed each other's company.

After the guide ended his tour, the two continued to walk and visited the rest of the attractions on the trail that weren't covered on the guided tour. They walked all afternoon and, when the sun set, they walked to the venue for Polly's show.

Flynn waited backstage and watched the performance. Polly played her best show ever, Flynn would tell her later.

After the show, a private car took them back to the hotel.

Flynn unlocked the door and gestured for Polly to go first. She entered the room and dropped her purse on a chair. She turned and waited for Flynn.

He shut the door and approached her.

Flynn smiled and cupped her jaw with his palm. He brushed his thumb over her cheek.

"I had fun today," he said.

She pressed her cheek into his hand. "Me, too."

"This was the best day I've had in a long time. Thank you."

His eyes met hers and she could see his happiness.

"Same."

Flynn leaned close and brushed his lips to hers, softly. Polly sucked his lip into her mouth. Flynn groaned and threaded his fingers into Polly's hair. He deepened the kiss. They kissed and nibbled and teased.

Polly lifted Flynn's shirt and slid it up his torso.

He broke the kiss. "How far do you want to take this?"

"All the way."

"Are you sure? Only if you're comfortable."

She kissed his tattooed chest, bared from lifting his shirt. "I'm sure. I want you, Flynn."

"Mmm, okay then."

Instantly, he peeled his shirt off and disposed of hers, too.

His hands wrapped around her hips, and his mouth pressed kisses to her neck.

He guided her toward the bed and slid their jeans off along the way.

She laid onto the bed when the back of her knees touched the mattress. Her legs still hung off the edge of the bed and her feet touched the floor.

Flynn kissed her stomach and dropped to his knees on the floor in front of her.

He pulled her legs over his shoulders and tugged her hips to the edge of the mattress. He thumbed aside her panties and swiped his tongue through her folds.

"Flynn," Polly breathed.

Flynn swirled his tongue around her clit and lapped at it. She moaned. He licked and sucked and caressed until she cried out wildly. He slid his tongue down to her entrance. Flynn swirled around it and licked it, thoroughly teasing her before he pushed his tongue inside. He plunged his tongue in and fucked her with it, then he brought his thumb up to stroke her clit.

"Oh god, Flynn." Her voice trembled and her fingers found his hair.

Flynn licked back to her clit and flicked it with his tongue. He slid two fingers inside her. He worshipped her clit and pumped his fingers until her legs began to shake around him and the pleasure overwhelmed her.

He gave her entrance one last swirl, kissed her clit, and stood.

Quickly, he stripped off her panties and dropped his boxers.

Polly sat up, which brought her face even with his thick, hard cock.

She pulled his hips toward her and opened her mouth. His cock slid between her lips and she sucked.

Flynn groaned and threaded his fingers into her hair.

She slid her lips as far up his length as she could go and brought a hand up to caress his balls.

"God, that's so good," he panted.

She bobbed her head and ran her tongue along the bottom of his length. Slowly she sucked and stroked him with her mouth.

"That's fantastic." He leaned his head back and panted. She kept licking and sucking. When he tilted his head forward, he said, "If you keep that up, I'm going to come. I don't want it to be in your mouth on our first time."

Polly gave one last suck then laid back on the bed. Flynn leaned in to ravage her mouth and he fit himself between her thighs. His body pressed over hers. Polly loved it. She could kiss this man forever, and the erotic taste of herself on his lips drove her wild. His cock brushed her slick entrance.

"I love you," he murmured against her lips.

"I love you, too," she panted.

Slowly, he slid his cock inside her. A delicious fullness made her moan as he stretched her in all the right places.

He kissed her as he bottomed out and stilled for her to adjust.

"You okay?" he murmured against her lips.

"Perfect."

Flynn began to thrust. She wrapped her legs around him and used them to press him closer. They were as close as two people could get, but she wanted more.

He burrowed his face in her neck and slid against her over and over as the two of them panted and moaned. Her hands traced up Flynn's back and went into his hair.

He slowed his strokes and leaned down to catch her nipple in his mouth. He sucked, licked, and kissed her breasts as he slowly fucked her.

Flynn's hand slid between them and rubbed her clit. His mouth left her breasts and consumed her mouth again. A desperate cry escaped her lips, which he cut off with a kiss.

"Come for me," he whispered against her lips then thrust into her.

Polly came and cried his name. Flynn's release hit him, too, and her walls fluttered hard around Flynn as he pulsed into her.

"Fuck yeah," he said. He pressed as far as he could into her and rested his sweaty forehead against her shoulder.

After a moment, he kissed her cheek and said, "I love you."

"I love you, too."

"I'll be right back," he said.

Flynn slid out of her, stood, and went to the bathroom.

Polly adjusted on the bed to rest her head on the pillows.

Flynn came back with a wet washcloth and walked beside the bed. "Open your legs for me," he said.

Polly did, and Flynn cleaned between her thighs with the soft, warm cloth. The sweet gesture made warmth grow in her chest. She felt treasured. He kissed her softly and smiled. "Give me a sec."

He tossed the used washcloth into the sink in the bathroom and came back to bed. He wrapped his arms around her as they spooned, her back to his front.

"Thank you for doing that with me. I've never gone bare with anyone before and it means the world to me that you wanted to do that," he said.

"What about Anika?"

He shook his head. "Deep down, I didn't trust her. Seems I was right. You're the only one. I trust you."

"I'm honored."

He kissed the back of her neck. "Get some sleep. We have a big day tomorrow."

"What do you have planned?"

"It's a surprise."

Chapter 17
Polly

"Welcome to Salem" the sign read as they drove by.

Polly turned to Flynn. "Are you serious?"

Flynn smiled. "Yep. Welcome to Salem."

"This is why none of your itinerary made sense."

Flynn laughed. "Maybe."

Flynn found a parking spot for their rental car and held her hand as they walked through the city.

They visited the Witch Dungeon Museum, the Witch House, the House of the Seven Gables, and the cemetery beside the Salem Witch trial memorials. They shopped in charming stores and even toured a life-sized pirate ship. Flynn bought her a beautiful necklace meant to repel negative energy, and she melted when he insisted on clasping it around her neck the first time.

"This is fantastic, Flynn. I never thought of coming here."

"I hoped you'd enjoy it. I know you planned to tour Boston, but I thought you could use a little magic, too."

They went into a cute, rustic restaurant and sat at a table in the back. They ordered a wood-fired pizza and settled in to wait. Luckily, none of the patrons recognized them.

"You flew in, right? Where did you fly from?" Polly asked. She took a drink of her sweet tea.

"Seattle. We played a show there a couple of days ago. We've got a few days down the east coast now before we break again."

"Did you sight-see around Seattle?"

Flynn smiled and shook his head. "No. I want to see it with you so I waited."

"Aww, Flynn. You should get out and see what you can. I don't know when I'll get to Seattle."

"I don't have the photographer's eye like you do. I have more fun sight-seeing with you. It'll be worth the wait. I intend to have dinner with you in the Lounge at the Space Needle sometime."

"I do want to visit there. I'll bet it's beautiful."

"We'll find out together."

The server brought their pizza, which smelled of delicious baked crust and alfredo sauce.

"One forest mushroom pizza. Roasted garlic alfredo sauce, arugula, wood fired mushrooms, and fresh mozzarella and romano. Enjoy."

"Thank you," Flynn said. The server turned and left. "This looks great."

"It does." Polly picked up a slice and took a bite. The alfredo sauce's flavor exploded on her tongue. She chewed and swallowed. "It *is* great. Dig in."

Flynn tried a bite of pizza and surprise at the delicious flavor flashed across his face.

They chowed down on the pizza and enjoyed the comfortable ambiance at the restaurant.

"Did the band have a problem that you missed sound check?" she asked.

"They were fine with it. I have to be back for the show but someone filled in for sound check."

"Good. What time do you have to be there for the show?"

"The opening band goes on at 7. I should probably be there around 8."

"Okay." Polly checked the time on her phone. "We should head back after this."

Flynn reached across the table and took Polly's hand. "Can we stay here, together, and not worry about going back to the real world? This is the happiest I've ever been, and I don't want to leave it."

She squeezed his hand. "Maybe someday. We can work toward this. Rockstar retirement? But for now we have to tour with the bands and go back to reality. We have contracts to honor and jobs to do. We can spend our time off together, though. And we won't be touring forever. We only have to get through it for a little while."

His gaze met hers. "Move in with me."

"Maybe."

He smiled. "That's not a no. I like my chances."

Polly smiled at him. "Let's get out of here. I get to watch you strut on stage then I get to leave with you. It's my lucky night."

* * *

Polly woke to the soft strum of an acoustic guitar. Flynn hummed along to it.

She rubbed her eyes and looked toward the sound.

Flynn sat on the room's couch in his boxers and played the guitar. He wore his glasses and wrote on music sheets in the dim lamplight. He must be working on new music.

Flynn noticed she'd awakened. "Sorry, I tried to be quiet."

"It's okay. What are you working on?"

He smiled. "Our duet."

Polly smiled back at him, sleepily. "How's it going?"

"Good. Almost done."

Polly blinked at him. Her eyes wandered over his muscles and tattoos. She'd never seen a sexier sight. How'd she get so lucky? "Those glasses are sexy, you know? I have to say I approve," she said.

He grinned and gestured for her. "Thank you. Come here."

Polly climbed from the bed and crossed the room to where Flynn sat. He put the guitar aside and pulled Polly into his lap.

He slung the guitar across her naked hips and wrapped his arms around her.

"Play something with me," he murmured. His lips brushed her ear.

"Okay. You strum."

Together, they played a sweet ballad. Polly formed the notes and Flynn strummed. They took turns softly singing the lyrics. He pressed soft kisses to her neck and shoulder as they played.

"I can't get enough of you," he said.

Polly rocked her hips against his growing hardness.

"I know what you mean."

"If you keep that up, I won't be able to concentrate on the music." He nipped the back of her neck.

"Maybe that's my point," she teased. She rocked against him again.

"Mmm, Polly."

Flynn adjusted his boxers and released his cock. Polly shifted her hips and lifted up far enough to sink down onto his length. They both whimpered when she fully seated herself.

"You feel perfect," Flynn murmured in her ear. "Ride me. Use me. Take what you need. Whatever you do, come hard for me." They played the guitar as they made love until they were too lost in each other to concentrate and they pushed the guitar aside.

Chapter 18
Polly

Polly smiled at the cameras as she and the rest of Lovely Oblivion sat on an elevated stage, behind a table decorated with sponsor logos and TV banners. Bulbs flashed and red lights glowed from the cameras pointed at them for the televised interview.

"Any new music coming soon?" one reporter asked.

Bex answered, "Well, as you know, we released an album earlier this year. We're still going strong and new music is in the works. Keep your ears open for new songs next spring."

"Polly, that video of you and Flynn Morgan playing together was fantastic. Can we expect more from you two?" a reporter shouted.

"We'll see what our record labels say. We don't have any plans right now, but who knows what the future holds," Polly said.

"How do you know Flynn Morgan?"

"Flynn and I met at a party a few years ago. We hit it off and became friends."

"Are you two dating?"

"No comment. That's not what this interview is about."

"Are you ladies pumped for the show tonight?" another reporter asked.

"Hell yeah," Jade answered. "We hope to see all your excited faces in the audience."

The interview continued for half an hour before the band said their goodbyes and left the table. They headed out to the waiting limousine.

"We've got an hour until the opening band starts," Greg said as they settled in. "There's catered food at the venue so the plan is to head there and hang out until showtime."

They arrived at the venue after a short drive and walked into the building to a big cafeteria-like room. Buffet-style pans lined a table at the front and the caterers removed the lids. Delicious scents tickled Polly's nose.

The band lined up to make plates. Bex made two — one for her and one for her husband — and excused herself to go have dinner with her husband and infant daughter on the bus.

Polly filled her plate with steaming food and sat at a table with the rest of the band.

"I think Bex wants to have some jam sessions on the bus so we can get ready for recording," Jade said after swallowing a bite of her food. "She said something about working on a new song she's got in mind while we're on the road tomorrow."

"That should be fun," their keyboardist, Maggie, said. "I can't wait to get back in the studio. I'm exhausted. And ready for this tour to be finished. I'd like to stay in the same place for a while. It will be nice to make some new music, too."

Jade said, "I'm tired, too, but I try to look at it from the perspective that we won't be doing this forever. Maybe a few more years of touring, then we'll exclusively have studio time. I know I definitely don't want to be one of the rockers still touring in my old age. This won't be long-term."

"True," Maggie said. "Doesn't make me any less tired."

Polly's phone rang as they laughed. She glanced at the screen and saw it was an unknown number so she quickly pressed ignore. Immediately, the number rang again. Again, she ignored it. When it rang a third time, Polly sighed and said, "Excuse me a second."

She answered the call and stepped out of the room, into the hallway.

"Hello?"

"Polly, it's me," Grady said.

She sighed and closed her eyes. "What do you want?"

"I want to say I'm sorry. I love you, baby. I was stupid and I made a mistake. What can I do to prove my love to you?"

Anger pulsed through Polly's veins. "You can't do anything. You hurt me. You devastated me. Not only did you cheat, you got *married* and had kids behind my back. You made me the other woman — and that should have been impossible because I was with you first! I will never forgive you."

"We can work this out."

"No. I'm with someone else now."

Grady scoffed. "Who? Flynn? That manwhore could never be loyal to anyone in his life."

"What the fuck ever. If that's the case, Pot meet Kettle. Flynn's an enormous upgrade. In more ways than one! You and I are done, Grady."

"We aren't done. I want to work this out. We're good together."

"I don't care what you want. We're done."

He sighed. "I didn't want to do this, but you need to come back to me, Polly."

"What?"

"I'll sell all your stuff and toss what I can't. Your travel souvenirs, your guitar collection, childhood mementos, everything. Gone."

"What?!" she shouted.

"You heard me. We belong together and I'll do anything to keep you from making this terrible mistake. I'll even forgive you for cheating with that floozy, Flynn."

Polly laughed. "You're delusional. You can't blackmail me into coming back to you. If you sell my shit, I'll sue the fuck out of you. We aren't together. I can't cheat on you. Fuck you. I regret wasting so much on you."

"Polly —"

She ended the call and blocked the number.

She drew a deep breath and stood with her back against the wall for a long time. She tried to tame the anger. How had she been with Grady for so long but had no idea how much of a jerk he was? Finally, when she had her emotions in check, she texted Flynn.

Polly: How was your day?

Polly shoved her phone into her pocket and returned to the table. Her band, her closest friends, sat there laughing and having a good time.

She sat down to eat her now-cold dinner and tried not to let Grady's words bother her. She was with Flynn. She wouldn't let her ex make her feel like she wasn't good enough.

Chapter 19
Polly

"Hold on, I'll be right there," Polly shouted from the hotel bathroom when a knock sounded at the door. Who could it be that early? It was only 8 am.

She put the hair dryer down on the counter and walked toward the door, her hair still damp from her earlier shower.

She looked out the peephole and squealed with surprise when Flynn grinned at her.

Polly pulled the door open.

"Flynn! What are you doing here?"

"Hi there." He stepped forward and kissed her. She returned the kiss and pulled him inside so they could shut the door.

He broke the kiss but kept his body pressed against hers. She repeated, "What are you doing here?"

"I had a day off and I thought I'd surprise you." Flynn brushed her hair away from her face and stroked his thumb down her cheek.

For the first time, she noticed Flynn didn't have any luggage.

"Where are your bags?"

"I can't stay long." He leaned in and his lips ravaged hers again. After a long, thorough kiss, he said, "I have a flight out on the red eye tonight so I didn't bring anything with me. I'm hoping to spend the day with you, then fly back to my band later. I needed to see you. I'm sorry I can't stay longer."

She smiled. "I won't complain. I'm happy to see you. What do you want to do? I don't know this town, but we have a few options. I was supposed to go shopping with the band. We can do that with them. You and I can go shopping. Or we can forget the shopping and stay here."

He laughed and kissed her. His hands slid down her curves to cup her ass. "Guess what my vote is."

Polly reached between them and gently traced his cock through his jeans. "I don't know. What's that?" she teased.

"Mmmm, I want you all to myself and I don't want to leave this room."

"Oh, yeah?"

"Mmmm, yeah."

"Okay. So online shopping?"

He laughed. "As long as I get to have my way with you first."

Polly blushed. "I have to tell the band to leave without me."

"Okay."

Flynn's lips found her neck, and she moaned as he trailed kisses along her throat.

He walked her backward to the bed, not stopping with the kisses. Flynn laid her onto the mattress and climbed over her. He pressed his hardness against her and rubbed his jeans teasingly against hers.

She whimpered at the delicious friction.

Polly. Plans. Cancel. Focus.

"Okay, hold on a second. Pause," she murmured.

He chuckled and kissed her, then supported his weight on his arms and leaned back. "Do what you need to do."

Polly pulled her phone from her pocket and fired off a quick text to the band's group chat.

Polly: I won't be attending today. Flynn surprised me and came here. I'm going to spend the day with him.

She tossed her phone toward the bedside table but heard it thud on the floor. She didn't care.

"Resume." She smiled.

Flynn grinned and pulled her shirt off. Immediately, he dove back in and peppered kisses down her neck, collarbone, and chest.

She gasped with pleasure when he tugged her bra aside and sucked a nipple into his mouth. He swirled his tongue over it, flicked it, and sucked it until she moaned and twisted her fingers into his hair.

"Oh, Flynn." She grinned deviously. "Master Flynn," she teased.

He let go of her nipple and grinned. His dimple winked at her. "Even though I'm not into master/sub play — unless you want to try it, I mean — hearing you say those words makes me unbelievably hard. I'll show you in a minute." He tugged her bra aside and teased her other nipple.

His hand moved between them and unfastened her jeans. One handed.

"That's not concerning at all," she murmured as her jealousy flashed.

He let go of her nipple and looked her in the eyes. "What?"

"Nothing. Continue."

"Polly."

She sighed. "You unsnapped my jeans easily one-handed. Made me think you have a lot of practice."

A smile touched his lips. "I have a past, you know that. But I promise I'm all yours now. Only yours. Anything that happened before you was practice — so you could have perfection. Okay? There's no one but you. I swear."

She believed him and pushed her jealousy aside. "Okay. I'm sorry. That was unfair."

He leaned back and sat on his knees. He slowly tugged her jeans over her hips and off her legs. He trailed kisses down her legs, following the trail of skin revealed by her jeans.

When the pants were off, he tossed them aside.

"You're beautiful," he said as he gazed at her in her matching underwear. Her breasts popped over her bra, and her hands rested above her head. "Fucking beautiful."

He glanced around and spotted her camera bag by her suitcase.

"Stay still," he said with a smile. He climbed off the bed and headed to her bags. He stripped out of his jeans and shirt along the way, and only wore his boxers when he grabbed her camera from the bag. Polly bit her lip and admired his strong tattooed frame.

He crossed the room and climbed onto the foot of the bed.

He turned her camera on.

She flushed. "Flynn, I know the camera is digital, so no one has to see the film, but I don't know how I feel about pictures like this."

"Don't worry. These are for my eyes only. No one else will ever see them, I promise. If it makes you feel better, I won't include your face in any naughty frames. ...Or if you don't want to do it, I won't."

She hesitated. It was a big risk for a celebrity to take nude photos. But she trusted Flynn. "Don't get my face, okay? That would make me feel better."

"Done."

He lined up the first shot, and she heard the shutter click.

"Gorgeous." He took a couple more shots.

He reached over and teased her nipples with his fingers, which had softened during their conversation, one at a time. Flynn groaned with appreciation as they re-hardened into peaks with his attention. He snapped a picture, then cupped one breast with his hand and slid a thumb over the hardened nub. He snapped a picture of his hand holding her breast.

She whimpered with pleasure, and his attention drew to her face. When he read her desire, he growled and dropped the camera aside on the bed.

He pressed his body against hers and kissed her. A deep, passionate, claiming kiss that left no doubt, Flynn considered her his. Over and over, for what seemed like hours, they kissed each other. "So lucky," he murmured.

His cock pressed against her folds through their underwear, and he rocked slowly against her. They both groaned.

Polly wrapped her legs around Flynn and pulled him closer. She sucked his bottom lip and ran her hands through his hair.

Flynn broke the kiss and looked at her, panting. He brought his hand up and traced her kiss-swollen lips.

"I love you," he said.

"I love you, too."

Flynn stepped off the bed and gripped her panties. He tugged them down her legs and pulled them off. He dropped them on the floor, and his boxers went next.

Before Polly knew it, Flynn pressed over her again, his warmth nestled against hers. She wrapped her legs around him and his cock nudged her entrance.

He ran his nose up her neck and sucked her earlobe into his mouth. He flicked and massaged it with his tongue. She shivered.

She pulled her nails down his back, and he made a groan of appreciation. He kissed along her jawline, then devoured her lips — desperate licks, sucks, and nibbles that drove them both wild.

"I love you," he murmured against her lips as he pushed his cock a few inches into her. He pulled back and thrust again, this time fully seating himself.

"Oh fuck. I love you, too," she said.

He made love to her. Slow, deep, rhythmic thrusts. She wrapped her arms around him and hugged him close as their sweat-slicked bodies moved together. They moaned and panted for what seemed like hours, not able to get close enough despite being joined but enjoying every moment of trying.

"Oh, yes," she breathed. She pulled her nails down his back and he gave a throaty groan. She felt the beginnings of an orgasm pulse around him. "Perfect."

He trailed kisses down her chest. When he sucked her nipple into his mouth and tugged, she lost it. She moaned loudly and pulsed around him in the strongest orgasm of her life.

"Fuck," he murmured. He pressed hard into her and spilled his come deep inside her. "You feel so good."

He wrapped his hands around her hips and rolled. He flipped them so that he laid on his back and she rested on top of him, his cock still firmly wedged in her.

She sat up and smiled at him from her seated position on his cock.

"What?" he asked with a smile, holding her hips with his hands.

Slowly, she rolled her hips. Flynn was still hard inside her.

He grinned. "Fuck yeah."

"Can you go again?"

He nodded. "Whenever you're ready."

Polly rocked her hips and rode Flynn. Her hips bucked against him and he drove up into her. Flynn's hands slid up her sides and found her breasts. He teased her nipples, and she threw her head back and rode him harder. He closed his eyes and pleasure washed over his face. "Oh yeah, Polly." They moaned and fucked until they both orgasmed again.

They both breathed hard as she tucked herself beside him on the bed. He wrapped his arm around her and rested his head against hers. The urge to turn over and sleep nagged her post-sex brain.

"Sex always makes me sleepy. I want to make the most of the day with you, though," she said. "I don't want to nap."

Flynn chuckled and pressed a kiss to her cheek. "It's okay if you need to sleep."

She shook her head. "No, I want to make the most of my time with you."

"It's okay if you nap. I understand. You have a show tonight. Plus, the bands' tours are almost over so pretty soon you'll move in with me and we'll get to see each other constantly."

She laughed. "I want to stay up. And I never said I'm moving in with you."

Flynn smiled as if it were a foregone conclusion. "You will." He kissed her.

They spent the rest of the day pumped up on caffeine and energy drinks. They had a leisurely day together, where they watched TV, played trivia together on their phones, and made love.

Polly walked onstage that night exhausted but happy, high on her unexpected time with Flynn. Lovely Oblivion played a fantastic show, then, when it was over, Polly crashed into her hotel bed and slept soundly, comforted because the sheets still smelled like Flynn.

Chapter 20
Flynn

"So what do you have planned for today?" Flynn asked. He held the phone to one ear and rummaged through the bus's mini fridge. He settled on a canned soda. He cracked it open one-handed then slid onto the bench seat of the built-in table. He slurped the cold cola into his mouth and swallowed.

"We have a radio interview this afternoon," Polly said. "I'm having lunch with Gideon first."

Flynn's stomach did somersaults as a wave of possessiveness hit him. "Gideon? As in Gideon Trent from the awards show?"

"Yeah. We're in the same city and he wants to talk about music. I figured it wouldn't hurt anything. Jade and I are meeting him for lunch."

Flynn sucked in a deep breath then released it. Different thoughts crossed his mind. Gideon was a player. Polly wouldn't be safe around him. He could steal her away. On the other hand, Polly was strong willed and wouldn't do anything with Gideon. She'd been cheated on before. And she was loyal. She wouldn't go there.

Ultimately, Flynn trusted her.

He rapped his knuckles on the table and made a decision. She was right; it wouldn't hurt anything. He and Polly both lived in the spotlight. This would happen again. He couldn't live in fear or be unfair to Polly.

He said, "I won't lie. I don't like him."

"I'm sorry. I can —"

"No," he interrupted. "Let me finish."

She stopped talking. "Okay, go ahead."

"I don't like him. But I trust you. I won't be a caveman. I hope you have a nice lunch today. Tell Jade hi for me."

Polly breathed an audible sigh of relief. "Thank you. Don't worry about Gideon. I'm all yours."

He smiled. "I know. I trust you."

"What do you have planned for today?"

"I'm on the bus all day. I'll be on the internet and playing video games." He lowered his voice. "Maybe looking at some of our naughty pictures later."

Polly laughed. "Oh yeah?"

"Oh yeah." Flynn laughed. "The sexiest woman in the world is mine and let me take risqué pictures of her. You bet I'm looking at those at every chance I get — and remembering what we did while taking them."

"Well you know, if you wait long enough, I can probably join you later."

Flynn cleared his throat. "Well then, I'm definitely calling dibs on the bus's bedroom tonight. Video chat?"

* * *

Polly

Lovely Oblivion sat inside the spacious radio studio, headsets with microphones on everyone.

"What type of sound can we expect on the new album?" the blond, female DJ asked.

"We have new songs but stay true to the sound our fans love," Bex said. "I think the new album will get a lot of love when it's released."

"Do you have a release date yet?"

"Not yet, but it will be next spring. Keep your ears open for the official date."

"Awesome, I will. Jade, Bex, fans are dying to know: what's it like having your significant other tour with you all the time?"

Jade laughed and said, "It's fantastic. I wouldn't have it any other way."

"I agree," Bex said. "I couldn't do this without my family, and I'm lucky enough to have the best of everything. My blood family gets to come with me and be one big unit with my adoptive family... My work family, because they really are family. I'm blessed."

"You ladies don't really get any breaks. Your home life and work life are combined. Is that extra stressful?"

"No," Jade said. "It's great. I get to do what I love with the people I love. I wouldn't change a thing. Except maybe my wedding date. I can't wait to marry Ryker and make this official." Jade laughed.

"Same. Except the marriage thing. Already took care of that." Bex laughed. "I wouldn't change anything about my life with Aiden. Like Jade said, I'm doing what I love with the people I love. I have a great life."

"That's fantastic. I'm happy to hear it. What are the next big plans for Lovely Oblivion?"

"Of course, the album release is coming soon, but we also plan to tour the U.S. again next year and there is some discussion about a global tour in the future," Bex said.

"That's exciting. Have you done a world tour before?"

"No, but that would be awesome. We would love to do it."

"Do you have any shows planned in the immediate listening area?"

"Our closest venue is about an hour away from your studio. It's not immediate, but it's close. We play tomorrow night if anyone wants to check us out."

"Would you ever consider playing our local venue?"

Bex said, "We'll play wherever the producers tell us to. Unfortunately, we don't have any control over that. We go where they book us. We would love to play a show here, but we don't get any say in the schedule. We hope to see all your faces at tomorrow's show, though."

"You heard it here, listeners. Get your tickets for tomorrow night's Lovely Oblivion show through the link on this station's website and get 20% off your purchase." The DJ made a wrap up signal. "Thank you for stopping by. We have to wrap this up. Where can listeners find more of your music?"

Bex said, "Check the Lovely Oblivion website for upcoming tour dates as well as links to our online music and social media."

"Thanks for stopping by. You've been listening to W03X with Lovely Oblivion." The DJ pushed some buttons and then said, "Okay, we are off the air. Thank you so much. The interview went great."

The band chatted with the DJ and stood to leave.

"Polly," the DJ said.

"Yeah?"

"The publicists told me not to ask on air but I'm dying to know. Off the record. What's up with you and Flynn Morgan?"

Polly blushed. "Off the record. We were friends for the past few years but now we are together."

The DJ grinned. "Right on." She high-fived Polly. "Is he really as much of a jerk as the news makes him out to be?"

Polly shook her head no. "He's one of the most thoughtful people I've ever met. The media gave him a bad boy image, but I don't see that side of him."

"Good. Best of luck to you two. You make a cute couple."

Polly smiled. "Thanks."

TABLOID NEWS
"Crossover"

Lovely Oblivion guitarist Polly Worthington and drummer Jade Lewis were photographed today having lunch with country music sensation Gideon Trent. The three appeared together for a friendly lunch and parted ways afterward. Rumors circulate that this may have been a business lunch. Is a crossover being planned? If it is, you heard it here. We will update as the news solidifies.

Chapter 21
Polly

Polly laid in her bunk and watched videos on her phone as the bus travelled to the next city. The latest episode of her favorite YouTube series streamed on her screen.

Lovely Oblivion only had a few shows left on this tour. She was exhausted and couldn't wait to settle in one place for the studio. Maybe afterward she would move in with Flynn like he kept asking.

A notification went off on her phone. She paused the video and checked the blinking icon. A google notification for Flynn's name. She navigated to the web page and clicked the link. The news was on a tabloid site, but it wouldn't hurt to see the latest rumor. Right?

The article was titled "Flamie?" Polly scrolled through the photos on the page, growing more nauseated with each one. Amie and Flynn sitting close together. Her face in his neck. Amie in his lap. His hand on Amie's breast. She didn't even have to read the tabloid's messed up story; the pictures said enough.

Polly's stomach sank. She knew it. Her worst fear had come true. Flynn couldn't handle the distance. He had turned to someone closer, someone who could be with him constantly. Her heart shattered when she realized that, despite his reassurances, in the end he'd turned to Amie.

Chapter 22
Polly

Polly stayed in bed and thought about it. It made sense. She and Flynn were hours apart. He was a man with needs. Of course he would indulge. Tears welled in her eyes and a wave of sadness hit her. They'd been doomed from the start. Their obligations would always keep them apart. The tears broke free. How Flynn handled this and how he'd let Polly find out was shitty, though.

The warmth from the tears flooded down Polly's cheeks as she tapped out a message on her phone.

Polly: We're done. No need to contact me.

The response was immediate despite the late hour.

Flynn: Whoa, wht hppnd? Answr the phne

Polly's phone rang. The familiar picture of Flynn's smiling face flashed across the screen. Her heart stuttered when she saw his picture, and she choked back a sob.

The voicemail notification lit up on her phone and text messages began pinging.

Polly turned off her phone and laid back in her bunk. The hum of the bus wheels and darkness surrounding her lulled her as she cried. The only light came from a muted TV built into the foot of the bunk.

She heard shuffling in the aisle outside and suddenly the bunk's barrier ripped back and Jade and Ryker's sleepy faces appeared. Jade's rainbow hair was sleep tossed and Ryker's dark hair was messy, like Jade had been running her fingers through it.

"What's wrong?" Jade whispered.

Polly sucked in a breath and started to answer but Jade nodded and interrupted. "Man trouble," Jade said.

Ryker nodded. "Okay, take the night to think about it. I'll arrange an assassination or kidnapping or whatever in the morning if you want. Hang on until daylight." He patted Polly on the shoulder. "I've got your back."

He turned to Jade. "Night, sweetness." He kissed her on the cheek, then disappeared into his bunk.

Jade chuckled and climbed into the bunk beside Polly and shut the curtain. "The perks of loving a SEAL." She snuggled up to Polly and wrapped her arms around her. Jade's warmth cocooned Polly. They touched noses and met eyes in the dim glow from the TV.

"Talk," Jade said.

"I - I..." Polly swallowed. "There are pictures of Flynn with his hands on Amie. I know the tabloids lie, but I didn't even have to read them. Pictures are worth a thousand words. His hands are on her. He knew that the two of them working together worried me." She sobbed. "He said it was a professional relationship. There's a picture with his hand on her boob. I don't see how that's professional."

"Oh, Polly." Jade hugged her tight. "I'm so sorry. If I can do anything, please let me know."

Jade stroked her hair and held her until they both drifted into a restless sleep.

In the morning, Polly woke before Jade. The warm body sleeping next to her was comforting, but it wasn't the one she wanted. She missed Flynn. But Flynn had betrayed her. She'd lost her best friend and her boyfriend at once.

Tears filled Polly's eyes. She'd trusted Flynn and never thought he would break her heart like this. Feelings of emptiness and hopelessness overwhelmed her. Every man she'd dated lied to her. Grady had been married. She'd asked Flynn about Amie and he'd told her nothing was happening. The lie made Flynn's betrayal sting worse than Grady's.

Polly turned on her phone, which lit up with missed calls and texts from Flynn. She deleted the texts without reading them and blocked his number. Polly couldn't bring herself to delete his voicemails. She wasn't perfect. What if she had a moment of weakness and needed to hear his voice one more time?

The bus no longer moved and her phone's clock showed that sound check would happen soon.

Lightly, she shook Jade, whose groggy eyes opened.

"Hey. You okay?" Jade asked.

"Yeah. It's going to take some time, but I'll be okay."

Jade nodded. "I'm here for you. If you ever want to talk or rant or whatever, you can come to me."

When Polly bobbed her head yes, Jade opened the curtain and hopped from the bunk. Polly followed her.

Ryker sat at the table up front with three steaming coffees in front of him. His short, dark hair looked neatly combed, and a tattoo poked out from the neck of his snug security shirt. He sipped his coffee.

Jade and Polly sat at the table with him and grabbed their coffees.

"Good morning," Ryker said. Jade smiled at him.

"Morning," Polly said.

"How's everything today?" Ryker watched Polly closely.

"Not great. But things'll get better, eventually," Polly said.

"Do I need to do anything?" He raised an eyebrow.

"No. I appreciate you asking but it's not necessary."

He drank his coffee and evaluated Polly over the cup rim. "Are you sure? I can make a face-to-face meeting happen if you want. My team would love a stealth extraction."

Tears welled up in her eyes. "I'm sure. I don't want to see him."

Ryker nodded. His eyes empathized with her. "You change your mind, let me know."

"I will."

He reached across the table and squeezed her hand. "Alternatively, I have a security team full of guys who would love to help you make his ass jealous." He grinned. "Roark would have a field day."

Polly laughed. "Maybe. I'll think about that."

He gave her hand another squeeze and let go. "We're here for you. You aren't alone."

The words were nice, but Polly couldn't help but feel quite the opposite.

"Thank you," she said.

Someone knocked on the bus door and within seconds, their tour manager, Greg, appeared through the curtain at the top of the steps. "Sound check in 15," he announced, pointing at Jade and Polly. "Tell the others." He disappeared and the bus door closed.

The group stood and headed back to the bunks to get ready for the day.

TABLOID NEWS
"Trouble in Paradise"

Though not officially announced, we suspected Late Nyght Smoke guitarist Flynn Morgan, and Lovely Oblivion guitarist Polly Worthington, also known as Flolly, to be dating. In unfortunate news for the rumored couple, Flynn was photographed in risqué photos with Late Nyght Smoke's songwriter, Amie Athey. Is the possibility of Flolly over now? Stay tuned for more updates.

Chapter 23
Polly

Lovely Oblivion had an amazing show. They did the meet and greets, press pictures, and all the requirements before returning to their bus that night.

Their guard for the night stopped Polly on her way onto the bus. "A florist dropped off flowers and chocolates. I put them on your bunk."

She grew queasy. "Thank you."

She climbed the bus steps and took the walk to her bunk apprehensively. A beautiful bouquet of white roses and a box of chocolates sat on the bed. Carefully, as though the card was a hand grenade rather than a piece of paper, she plucked the note from the bouquet. Behind it was the picture of them wearing mismatched clothes before the awards show.

The note read:

Polly, Please talk to me. The pictures aren't what they look like. I promise. Please let me explain. I love you. I would never hurt you on purpose. Love, Flynn.

Tears welled in her eyes. How could it not be what it looked like? Obviously, the camera caught them in an intimate moment Flynn had never wanted Polly to see and he wanted to back pedal.

She blinked back the tears. She carried the flowers and chocolates to the kitchenette and threw them in the trash. With no shame, she held onto the picture. Maybe it was the last picture she would ever have of them together. She couldn't bring herself to toss it.

She returned to her bunk, put the picture into her storage drawer, and climbed inside. She turned on some music and shut her eyes. Maybe she could sleep the hurt away.

A text message chimed on her phone. She opened her eyes and checked. Unknown number.

Unknown: It's Flynn. I nd to tlk to u. Pls cll me

Flynn. Her breath caught and tears rolled down her cheeks. Immediately, she blocked the number.

She heard the rest of the band climb onto the bus, laughing and carrying on. She tried to put Flynn out of her mind and joined her friends in the front lounge for an exciting, rockstar night of board games.

* * *

Polly ran offstage after the show and handed her guitar to a roadie.

"Thanks, man," she said, wiping the sweat off her face with her hand.

"Great show," he said and took the instrument.

"Thanks," she said.

"Polly," a familiar voice said from behind her. Her heart leaped. Then she remembered she was mad at him.

She turned and saw Flynn standing there. Nausea hit her when she saw how rough he looked. His hair was messy, and he had days' worth of scruff on his face. He hadn't shaved. Frown lines creased his forehead. He appeared stressed and disheveled, like he was falling apart and didn't know what to do. For a second, her heart went out to him; she reigned in her sympathy and fixed a passive expression on her face.

"Flynn," she said and turned to walk away.

"I need you to listen to me. I can't lose you."

"You should've thought of that earlier," she said and stepped away.

Arms around her waist stopped her. Flynn rested his face on her shoulder and hugged her from behind. She froze.

"I didn't do anything," he said. "Polly, this is killing me. Nothing happened. I can't lose you, especially over something I didn't do."

She drew a deep breath, shook her head, and said, "I saw the pictures. They're pretty damning."

She felt Flynn shake his head no. "Amie was drunk. I wasn't. She fell onto my lap and I grabbed her to keep her from tumbling onto the floor. I guess my hand ended up on her chest in the chaos. I don't know. I grabbed without noticing where. I don't even know. Someone snapped pictures right then. That's all it was. An innocent moment blown out of proportion. I told Amie a long time ago that I belong to you so she and I could work together, but that's it. I swear nothing happened. Nothing will happen. You're the only one for me." He squeezed her tight and inhaled her scent desperately.

"Problem here?" Ryker approached, intimidating in his security shirt. He looked them up and down.

Flynn hugged her once more, sadly as though it would be the last time, then reluctantly let go.

"No," he said. "I've said my piece. I'll leave now so Polly's got some time to think about it."

Ryker nodded at Flynn. "Sounds like a good idea."

Flynn pressed a kiss to Polly's cheek.

"I love you. Take some time to think about what I said." He hesitated, then added, "I miss you."

Her heart ached with his admission. She missed him, too.

Flynn disappeared before Polly even turned around.

"You okay?" Ryker asked.

"Yeah. Flynn wouldn't hurt me."

A small smile played across Ryker's lips. "He wouldn't, huh?"

"No."

"I'm glad to hear you say that."

Ryker put his hand on her elbow and pulled her to the side of the walkway as some crew went by.

"Listen. I know you didn't ask for help, but I had some witness interviews done with people who attended that party," he said.

She glared. "And you found out he was hanging on Amie all night?"

Ryker gave her a sad smile and shook his head. "The opposite, actually. Amie does have her sights on Flynn; you were right. But multiple people said Flynn actively discourages her if she tries anything and does not reciprocate. At the party, Amie got drunk and repeatedly hit on Flynn. He told her, in front of a crowd, that she was being disrespectful to his girlfriend and needed to be professional or he would no longer work with her."

Tears flooded Polly's eyes. She blinked them back. Had she jumped to conclusions?

Ryker extended his arms out for a hug and motioned for her to come to him. When she did, he enveloped her in a warm embrace. Polly didn't have siblings, but she knew a brotherly hug when she felt one.

"There's more. Are you ready?" he asked.

She nodded against his chest.

He said, "The photos were a drunken mishap that lasted seconds. Someone snapped those pictures at an opportune time." He took a step back and looked at Polly. "Amie literally fell. Flynn caught her, set her on her feet, told her to straighten her shit up, and it was done. He probably didn't even think twice about it until the pictures showed up. For the record, Amie is gone from Late Nyght Smoke. Flynn asked Miguel to remove her for her unprofessional conduct right after the party, before you even saw the pictures. Turns out, Amie had sex with Will and made moves on the other band members. She was trying to catch any 'big fish' she could, any way she could. I hope Will was smart, or he's probably going to have a paternity lawsuit pending. I trust my source. Flynn did right by you; the pictures lied."

A sob escaped Polly's lips. Ryker pulled her into another hug and soothed her.

"It seems to me," he said, "you should go to the Hilton and visit room 301. You and Flynn have some things to work out."

"Wait, how do you — you knew he was here?"

Ryker smiled. "He was here when the bus pulled in this morning. My source hadn't gotten back to me yet about the party, so I made him wait before I let him near you." Ryker chuckled. "I've got your back. Making Flynn wait this long to see you took three guards. The man misses you. Give him a chance."

Polly shook her head. Her thoughts turned to Grady. "Maybe he didn't lie now, but everyone I love lies and leaves me. It's only a matter of time. I might as well stay alone now and save everyone the trouble."

Ryker stepped back and narrowed his eyes at her. His military background peeked through and he adopted the cutting tone often associated with military discipline. "Well, congratulations, you set a record. That's the biggest load of shit I've ever heard. I should get you an award."

"Wh - what?" Tears flowed down Polly's cheeks.

His serious tone didn't change. "Grady was an asshole. But because he treated you like shit doesn't mean everyone will. None of this self-pity nonsense. It's in your head. It's not true. Key example is: Flynn adores you. That man loves you, and it's obvious with every move he makes. Did you know he's supposed to be at his own show right now but he skipped it to be here for you?"

She sobbed. "Really?"

"Yes." Ryker blinked a few times and put away his military side. He pulled her into another hug and let her cry on his shoulder. "I'm sorry. That slipped. I was in the SEALs for too long. Look, you know I'm here for you. You've become like a sister to me. I don't know where you got these ideas, but I want to stop them now. They are untrue. You are worthy. You are loved. You are treasured. I talked to Flynn myself before I considered letting him in here. He loves you and he wants to do right by you. None of those fears you expressed are going to happen. They're unfounded. You should give him a chance." Ryker leaned back and smirked. "Plus, if he fucks up, I'll torture him. You can help."

Polly laughed. "Why does it sound like you want him to fuck up?"

Ryker grinned. "There's the woman I know. Hello, Polly. Now, do you want to hear Flynn out?"

She drew a deep breath and nodded.

"Excellent. Hang on, one of my guys'll take you. Room 301."

"Got it."

Chapter 24
Polly

Polly knocked on door 301.

Ryker sent a bodyguard to drive her to the hotel. She'd asked him to wait in the car and he'd ignored her request, but at least he'd waited in the lobby.

She stood alone in the hallway in front of Flynn's door.

After a minute, the door opened, and Flynn appeared in front of her.

"Polly?" he asked. He stared at her like he wasn't sure it was really her.

"Can I come in?"

"Of course, please." He stepped aside to let her in.

She stepped through, and the door closed behind her. She turned to face Flynn. He watched her anxiously, like he wasn't sure how she would act. He leaned back against the wall and pressed his hands flat behind him as he watched her.

"I'm sorry," she said. "I should have listened to you."

"No, I'm sorry," he whispered. "The first place your mind jumped when something happened was the possibility that I'd done it. I obviously did something wrong if you doubt me."

What? No.

She shook her head and said, "It's not you. You've been great. But I've had so much self-doubt since Grady. I've felt like damaged goods. Like no one could want me." She blinked back tears.

Flynn scoffed, but didn't move from his spot against the wall. "Not true."

"I know."

"I was a shitty friend and even shittier boyfriend if you ever believed that. Nothing could be further from true."

She hated that he would take the blame like that when it was clearly her fault. He'd done nothing wrong.

"All I'm saying is my self doubts got us into this mess. I'm sorry I overreacted." She sniffled and focused on him. His hands were still behind his back. "Why are you standing like that?"

"I don't trust myself not to touch you. You're still in your stage clothes, which I find practically irresistible, and I haven't been intimate with you for a while. I'm trying to stay out of trouble."

Polly stepped toward him.

"You don't have to do that. I'm sorry, Flynn."

He didn't move, but his gaze met hers. She stopped walking.

He said, "I needed you to talk to me, Polly. If you were having doubts about anything. About me. About us." He shook his head. "I lost my closest friend and the woman I love at the same time over something I couldn't control. A stupid mistake. And I couldn't even explain because the person I respect the most in this world — you — doubted me. It doesn't feel good."

Polly shook her head. Tears broke free and streamed down her cheeks.

Flynn continued, "Look at me, I'm a mess. A few days without you... I already look homeless, and I backed out on a concert. But none of it matters knowing that you're done with me."

"I'm not done with you." The fact that she'd made Flynn feel so badly about himself tore her apart.

Flynn shook his head. "You blocked me, Polly. Even if you aren't done with me now, you were before. I want to be with you. I want you to trust me. I love you. After all this, though, I don't know if we can make a relationship work. We'd have to trust each other. People manipulate our lives every day to look how they want through the press. They lie. They blow insignificant moments out of proportion. Then the distance and separation will always be factors. I don't know if we can move past the way things look and the half truths of the press when we're apart. Maybe we can only ever be friends."

Polly sobbed. "We can work on it. We can promise to always talk any problems out first. I'm sorry. Please give me another chance. I want to be with you. Do you still want to be with me?"

"Of course I do."

"Will you work on it with me?"

Flynn nodded. "I want to, more than anything."

Polly launched herself at Flynn and wrapped her arms around him.

Flynn removed his hands from the wall and hugged her. He buried his face in her neck.

"I love you," she said.

"I love you, too," he murmured against her throat.

"I'm sorry. I was wrong."

Flynn chuckled. "Well, there's one for the record books."

She lightly smacked him.

He kissed her cheek. "Can we lie down? I need to hold you."

"Please."

"Do you want to shower first? I think there's a robe in the bathroom. I don't care either way, but I thought you might want to take off the leather pants."

Polly looked down and laughed. "Good idea. Come on, big guy. You're coming with me. Let me text Ryker to call off the security guard downstairs and then you should help me out of my stage clothes."

* * *

Polly's phone woke her the next morning. She wiggled out from beneath Flynn and stretched her arm to grab the phone off the bedside table.

She turned off the alarm, rubbed her eyes, and checked her messages. She had text message notifications from Ryker.

Ryker: The bus is on the way to Cleveland. You play there Tuesday — two nights from now. Flynn is supposed to be in Richmond tomorrow. Get your ass to Cleveland in two days and

Flynn to Richmond tomorrow. My guard, Diesel, is still there and will help. Reach out to him ASAP. I'll text his #

Polly laid her phone aside and turned to Flynn. He'd turned on his back and rested with his mouth open, though no snores came out. She loved the youthful look that sleep created on his face, as much as she loved the strength beneath his tattoos. Flynn was a mix of everything — whimsy, fun, strength, and steadiness.

They'd had amazing makeup sex in the shower last night. When they'd gone to bed, Flynn had simply held her. She'd slept so well in his arms. It had been a great night.

Polly tugged the cover off and tossed it aside. She shifted on the bed so that she knelt between his legs. She closed her mouth over his hard, thick morning wood and slid down.

Flynn moaned in his sleep but didn't wake.

She kept going, sliding up and down slowly.

Flynn's hand reached out to the back of her head and his eyes fluttered open.

"Fuck yeah. Wake me up like this anytime," he said and groaned.

Her lips left his cock with a pop and her tongue swirled his balls.

"Oh yeah," he whispered.

She sucked one into her mouth and massaged it with her tongue, lightly sucking and tugging, then she switched to the other. She swirled her tongue on the skin between them, then over each of them. Her hand went to his cock and stroked it while she teased him. He grew harder under her attention.

She licked up the bottom length of his cock and slid her mouth onto it. She bobbed up and down.

Flynn fisted her hair and moaned. She sucked her cheeks in and hugged him with her mouth. She bobbed up and down and licked him as his breathing deepened and he guided her head with his hand.

"I'm coming," he warned.

Polly sucked and licked that much harder. Flynn groaned loudly and released into her mouth.

She swallowed and teasingly kept sucking.

He laughed, bit his lip, and made an uncomfortable noise. "God, that feels good, but it's sensitive right now."

Polly laughed, pulled her lips off with a teasing "pop", and scooted up the bed beside him.

He turned to face her. "Hi," he said with a smile.

He brushed her hair away from her face and tucked it behind her ear.

"Hi," she answered.

He softly kissed her, then he hugged her close and said, "Good morning."

"Good morning."

"That was the best wake up I've ever had. Thank you."

"You're very welcome."

"What do you have to do today?" Flynn ran a hand over his face.

Polly kissed his jaw.

"We can spend today together, but you have to get to Richmond for a show tomorrow. I have to be in Cleveland on Tuesday."

Flynn groaned and buried his face between her breasts. "Do I have to go to Richmond? Can I pay someone to take my place in the band and I travel with you instead?"

Polly smoothed his hair. "Your band probably wouldn't like that. There are only a few more shows on this tour, anyway. It sucks but we can do it."

Flynn raised his head and looked into her eyes. "Are you moving in with me when our tours are over?"

"Do you really want me to?"

"Of course."

She looked at his earnest face, which anxiously awaited an answer. His green eyes looked worried. How could she say no to that face?

"Okay," she said. "I'll move in with you."

Flynn grinned and kissed her. "Yesssssss," he said.

Polly said, "We still have probably two or three months before I can move in, so don't get too excited. I have studio time in New York after my tour. Your house is in Oregon. I can't move across the country until studio time is done."

Flynn frowned. "I don't like it. You'll be too far away."

Polly ran her fingers through his hair. "I'm sorry. Studio time has been booked for months for our next album. You know how hard it is to get recording time."

Flynn's frown turned into a smile. "Do you have a place rented yet?"

"Yeah, I do."

"Want some company while you're staying there?" He looked at her hopefully.

Her heart stuttered. He would move, even temporarily, for her? Touring, they got minimal time at home, anyway, but if Flynn kept her "company" then he was offering to spend the time that Polly recorded away from home so he could be with her.

Flynn must have read her face because he said, "I enjoy my house and I like to be there when I can, but it's only a house. I guarantee I will be happier living with you. Wherever you need to be. Being with you is the most important factor to me right now."

He locked his gaze with hers, pulled her hand to his lips, and kissed it.

"Okay," she said. "Want to come stay with me in New York?"

Flynn grinned and kissed her. He whispered against her lips, "Yes," then continued kissing her.

Chapter 25
Polly

Polly watched Flynn perform from backstage. In person, the current felt even more electric than the streamed shows she'd watched. The beat of every song hummed through her body, and she moved and sang to all of them.

Mid-set, Flynn gestured to Will and spoke into the microphone. A quick glance backstage at her revealed his plan.

He said, "How about it, everyone? Tonight, we have a special guest backstage. Maybe if you're really nice, she'll come out and sing for you."

The crowd cheered wildly. A chant of her name began.

Right as Polly wondered what was happening, a roadie ran up and handed her a guitar and onstage earpieces, which would protect her ears from the roar of the crowd. She swung the guitar strap over her shoulder, put in the earpieces, and walked onstage. The roar and whistles of the crowd grew impossibly louder.

She approached Flynn and spoke into his stand-up microphone. "It's a good thing it was me or y'all would have felt awful silly."

The chant of her name grew even louder.

Flynn put his arm around her shoulders and kissed her temple. "Thank you. I'm sorry to put you on the spot. I thought this would be fun."

Polly kissed him and the audience went insane.

Flynn chuckled. "Thanks for clearing up any speculation. That officially announced us as a couple to the public."

"That's okay with me."

"Good." Flynn squeezed her ass. "Do you know how to play *Mine*?" he asked.

Polly nodded. "Yes."

"Awesome. Let's play that. I'll sing with you."

Flynn ran around the stage and told his band the plan. When he was done, he stepped back to his microphone and said, "We don't play this song live very often, so you are in for a rare treat. Also, please forgive us if we're rough because this is a surprise. We're winging it and haven't rehearsed. Polly and I are going to sing a duet for you."

The crowd cheered and cell phone cameras were raised to capture the moment.

They played and sang the band's heart-wrenching duet beautifully, with only a few minor mess-ups. When the song ended, Polly bowed, kissed Flynn, and ran offstage.

She handed the guitar to a waiting roadie, then stood by the curtains to watch the rest of the show.

Late Nyght Smoke rocked their set and had the crowd chanting after their last song.

Polly high-fived each of them and congratulated them on a great show as they came offstage.

Flynn handed his guitar off for safe keeping then set his sights on Polly. He grinned and wrapped his arms around her. He picked her up in a hug and spun them in a circle.

"Great show," she said as he sat her on her feet.

"Thank you. You did fantastic on *Mine*."

His eyes flicked to her lips. She licked them in anticipation. Flynn leaned in to kiss her, but before their lips touched, Diesel, the bodyguard, stepped forward. With his buzz cut blond hair and an eagle tattoo on his forearm, Diesel screamed former military.

"Sorry," he said. "Polly, we have to leave in ten minutes for our flight."

"Okay, thanks," she said.

Diesel nodded and walked away.

Flynn hugged her close and pressed his forehead to hers. "I don't want you to go," he said.

"I don't want to go either."

He sighed. "Only a few more shows. We've got this." He kissed her. "Thank you for going public with our relationship. It means a lot to me."

"You thank me now. Wait till we hear from PR tomorrow. They'll be pissed that they weren't involved."

Flynn chuckled.

"They'll lecture. I don't care. It doesn't bother me," he said. "I love you."

"I love you, too."

He hugged her tight. "Thank you for coming to the show. I enjoyed spending the past couple of days with you."

"Same. Chin up. It won't be long until we can be together every day in New York."

Flynn growled. "Right. And then maybe next year we'll tour together and not have to worry about separation."

"I hope."

"I'm working on Miguel. You work on Paige. We've got this." He kissed her temple.

"We've got this."

TABLOID NEWS
"Love Triangle"

Late Nyght Smoke guitarist Flynn Morgan, and Lovely Oblivion guitarist Polly Worthington officially announced themselves as a couple at Late Nyght Smoke's latest concert — but how long has this relationship happened outside the public eye? Polly and Flynn sang the band's infamous love duet together onstage and shared several lip-locks during the performance, proclaiming their relationship.

But has their torrid affair been happening for years? Polly's ex-fiancee, Grady McClelland, exclusively stated that Polly and Flynn have likely dated for years. He says, "They were both on the road, but Polly saw Flynn every time she had a chance. The two have known each other for years and often spent nights together at their hotels. I tried not to let it bother me because I loved Polly so much and she always said they were only friends. But now I'm not so sure. She moved on fast. I think she cheated on me with Flynn for years."

You heard it here first, folks. Were Polly Worthington and Flynn Morgan part of a love triangle?

Chapter 26
Polly

"Yeah, he sold it all," Polly said into the phone as she stood at the counter of Flynn's kitchen. "All my childhood mementos, my clothes, souvenirs, everything. Grady held a big auction and sold it all. Including my guitars and camera lenses. He probably made thousands. Maybe hundreds of thousands with the guitars."

"That rat bastard," Paige growled.

"Everything I had in our house together is gone. I'm basically starting over."

"I'm so sorry. That's awful. We can probably sue him."

Flynn walked up behind Polly, wrapped his arms around her waist, and kissed the back of her neck. She slid her hand over Flynn's.

"I don't think I want to. I want to be done with Grady and put that part of my life behind me. Plus, it wouldn't get my stuff back."

Paige sighed. "Understandable. Let me know if you change your mind. I'd love to sue that asshole. I'd handle it for you."

Polly laughed. "Thanks, Paige."

"You're welcome. Talk soon." Paige made a kissy noise and hung up.

Polly shoved her phone in her jeans pocket.

"Everything okay?" Flynn asked as he hugged her.

"Yeah, I was telling Paige about what Grady did. I still can't believe it."

"He's a moron. His loss was my gain, though." He kissed her cheek. "I need to thank him for ruining his chances with you."

She blushed. "Thank you. I'm definitely happy with how things worked out."

Flynn kissed a line down her neck.

She glanced out the window and watched as a construction worker walked out of the pool house.

"You've still never told me what's going on out there," she said.

"A few renovations," he murmured. "They'll be done soon."

"What renovations?"

Once Lovely Oblivion had finished in the studio, Polly moved in with Flynn at his house in Oregon. Polly hadn't had much to move, but Flynn had insisted on jointly picking some new furniture and he'd had a few of her photos enlarged and mounted in frames he'd hung around their house. He'd done everything he could to make her feel like it was her home, too.

He smirked. "You'll see."

Flynn's house — their house — had a combined kitchen and living room. A kitchen island separated them. The ceiling was sky-high, the entire height of the house. An upstairs balcony overlooked the rooms from the side. A hallway entrance stood underneath the balcony, which led back to the music studio, bathroom, and stairway upstairs to the bedrooms. Awards and band photos hung on the walls of the studio. It also housed a piano and their guitar collection — as guitarists, the collection was becoming extensive.

Flynn took her hand and led her to the couch in the living room. They sat down and snuggled together on the couch. Flynn used the remote to turn on the TV. He flicked through the channels until he reached one that played the *Boondock Saints*.

"Okay with you?" he asked.

"That's fine."

They snuggled and watched the movie together in silence, until someone knocked at the front door.

"I'll see who it is. Be right back," Flynn said. He kissed her forehead and climbed from the couch. He headed to the front door.

Polly could hear low voices but couldn't tell what they talked about. Flynn said, "Thank you," and closed the door. He pressed his back to the door and looked at Polly with a smile. He gestured for her to come to him.

She climbed off the couch and went to Flynn. She wrapped her arms around his waist and rested her head against his chest. His steady heartbeat thudded beneath her ear.

He hugged her and pressed a kiss to her hair.

"I have a surprise for you," he said.

"Oh, yeah?"

"You're going to love it." He squeezed her, then nudged her into the house. She let him guide her and he directed her toward the back door.

Flynn opened the door, and they stepped outside on to the warm concrete patio. The evening concrete was hot but tolerable under their bare feet. Potted plants and comfy chairs surrounded a fire pit. Beyond lay the pool and lounging chairs, which led to the gray pool house.

Flynn's arm wrapped around Polly's shoulder and tucked her into his side. They walked to the pool house, which had darkened and stood empty. A breeze blew and made the waves lap against the pool.

"I wanted to surprise you. I hope you like it." Flynn smiled at her and punched the key code to open the pool house lock. He swung the door open, and they stepped inside. Everything looked normal to Polly as she glanced around the compact living room and kitchen.

"The surprise is upstairs," Flynn said with a smirk.

Polly playfully glared at him and they walked down a hallway with closed doors to the bathroom and guest room, then climbed the stairs.

The door at the top of the stairs was new. There was also a small box that appeared to be a light mounted on the wall beside the door.

"Open the door. Go inside," Flynn encouraged.

Polly swung the door open and turned on the light switch.

"Flynn..." she said as she looked around.

"Check it out." He kissed her temple and grinned.

They'd once used the upstairs as a large studio-style game room. The space had been converted to a large photography darkroom, complete with beautiful counters, shelves, a sink, a developing station, and a photo drying space. The windows were blacked out and the only light came from the overhead lights in the room.

Flynn pointed to the light switch. "There's a button here that will turn on the light in the hallway. If you have things dark in here developing photos, you can turn on a signal in the hallway from that button. That way anyone outside knows you're working and none of your photos accidentally get light exposure."

Flynn wrapped his arms around her waist and pulled her close.

"This is just the beginning," he said into her ear. "You can customize it however you want."

"This is perfect. You didn't have to do this. Thank you."

He kissed her neck. "Yes, I did. You deserve your own space for your passions. This is your home, too. We can do whatever we want. Think about it."

He trailed kisses up her neck then brought his lips to hers. His soft lips devoured hers, as always. He could never seem to get enough.

He broke the kiss and pulled her into a tight hug. "I hope you like it."

"I do. Thank you."

Flynn bent her over one of the new counters.

She heard him say, "Let's give this place a proper christening."

Flynn unbuttoned her jeans. He slid the denim and her panties off her hips. She gasped when he dropped to his knees and his tongue found her pussy from behind. She spread her legs and Flynn worshipped her with his tongue.

When her legs began to shake, Flynn stood, released his cock, and pushed into her with one thrust. Flynn pushed fully against her and raised her up so they stood fully pressed together, him fully seated inside her.

He kissed her ear and murmured, "You ready?"

"I am. Take me hard."

He stayed lodged in her and pressed her down so she was bent over the counter. He slid his hands under her shirt, up her back. He rubbed them along her back and over her ass. Then he slapped her ass cheek, hard enough it would leave a red handprint. The momentum made her shift along his length and she moaned. He stroked where he slapped, soothing it.

Flynn began moving slowly in and out of her, and he built up the thrusts until he pounded her. His hands circled her hips and helped move their hips together.

"Yes, harder," she panted.

He drilled into her. The cabinets lining the counter pounded with their motions. He slipped a hand around her and stroked her clit.

She cried out loudly. "Oh fuck, Flynn. I'm going to come. Keep going."

She grew slicker as he pounded her, his fingers expertly playing her clit like a guitar. She felt her inner walls begin to flutter around him. Her release let go hard and she moaned. Her pussy clenched him.

Flynn groaned and jerked. His warmth flooded inside her. He leaned his body over her back and rested against hee, still lodged in her.

"That gets better every time," he panted.

Polly laughed. "I'm glad to hear you say that. We have more counters to christen."

Chapter 27
Polly

Eight months later

Will, the lead singer of Late Nyght Smoke, riled up the crowd and had them chanting and clapping as Polly watched from behind the curtains. She clapped along and catcalled the band, which earned her grins from each of the guys.

Late Nyght Smoke had released their new album that summer, but Flynn and Polly had written the songs. She thought they'd found a middle ground, which let them stay true to the band's sound but also bring in new fans. They'd also included Flynn and Polly's duet on the album — the ballad had been a hit. Their album had hit the top ten within the release week and stayed there steadily.

Polly and Flynn's bands unfortunately hadn't been able to tour together that year, but she and Flynn adopted a "one week" rule — they never spent more than a week apart. Whichever one of them had a day off flew to see the other wherever they were on tour. They also did movie nights over the phone on Tuesdays when they were apart. They made the best of the long distance, and hoped to tour together, eventually.

After the song ended, one of the road crew carried a chair to center stage, placed it, and ran off.

Polly frowned. That wasn't usually part of the show. Usually, they played their last song at this point.

"You're in for a treat tonight," Will said into the microphone. Cheers and applause went up.

"Polly," a tiny woman wearing a headset said from beside Polly, which made her jump. She handed Polly stage earpieces. "Please join them onstage."

"Wh-" Polly began, but she glanced up and saw Flynn gesture for her. She started to put in the earpieces. "What's going on?"

"Don't worry, honey. Get out there," the woman said with a smile. Then she turned and ran off.

What in the world?

Polly finished inserting the earpieces and walked toward Flynn. He approached the chair. She didn't have a guitar. Did they want her to sing?

The crowd went wild when Polly appeared onstage. She raised her hands in the air and waved in acknowledgment.

Flynn motioned for her to sit in the chair, which she did. She faced directly toward the packed crowd.

Flynn kissed her hair. "I know you're wondering what's going on. You'll see in a minute."

Flynn began playing a slow song on his guitar. The rest of the band soon joined in. He started singing and crooned slow, soulful lyrics about eternal love and life. Her heart pounded in her chest. What was going on? She'd never heard this song before and Flynn so rarely sang.

Flynn sang the sweet lyrics and skillfully played the slow guitar riffs. Tears filled Polly's eyes as she listened to the lyrics of the love song. It was beautiful. Did Flynn write this? Did he really feel this way? About her?

"I love you," she mouthed to Flynn when he glanced back at her.

He smiled and kept singing.

The words ended and Flynn backed away from the microphone. He faced her and expertly strummed the last riff on his guitar. She clapped along with the audience.

As the last note rang out, Flynn dropped to a knee in front of Polly. His clear green eyes peered up at her hopefully.

"Polly, you mean everything to me. In front of all these people, I promise you my love and loyalty. We aren't perfect, but that's okay because we're perfect for each other. I would be honored if you would agree to spend your life with me. Will you marry me?"

He pulled something from behind his guitar. He held a black box up to Polly and opened it to reveal a beautiful diamond ring.

She gasped. She loved this man but this proposal was completely unexpected. He really had surprised her. Tears of happiness streamed down her face. "Yes," she said.

Flynn grinned and slid the ring onto her finger. "Yessssss." He kissed her.

The crowd roared. Flynn took Polly's hand and pulled her out of her chair. He held their hands together in the air in celebration as they walked offstage. The crowd ate it up. A chant of "Flolly" began. The rest of the band bowed and wrapped up the performance for the night.

Flynn leaned his guitar against a speaker, then pressed Polly against a nearby wall and kissed her. He tangled his fingers into her hair and fused his mouth with hers. He pressed his body close to hers, and Polly enjoyed the feel of his warmth and pressure against her.

Polly loved every minute. With Flynn, she felt like they could rule the world and accomplish anything, side by side. She knew that she and Flynn would find the best way to be perfectly imperfect together.

TABLOID NEWS
"Fairytale Wedding"

On Saturday, Late Nyght Smoke guitarist Flynn Morgan, and Lovely Oblivion guitarist Polly Worthington (also known as "Flolly") tied the knot in a fairytale wedding in Paris, France. The couple and their private guestlist kept the night ceremony a secret until the wedding, a small miracle. Flolly kept the night magical with decorative lighting, music, and custom vows in front of the Eiffel Tower. The photos prove that it was indeed a fairytale wedding. There are also rumors of a baby Flolly in the works. Keep checking back here for the latest news.

AUTHOR'S NOTE

Reviews are really important for independent authors. Please consider leaving a review if you enjoyed the book. Just a line or two would mean a lot.

Thank you!

Thank you for reading Polly's story!
Stay tuned for more Lovely Oblivion in Book 4!

BOOKS

Lovely Oblivion: Jade (Book 1):
A rockstar/bodyguard suspense romance

Lovely Oblivion: Bex (Book 2):
A second chance romance

If you haven't read Lovely Oblivion: Jade yet, check it out on Amazon!
Chapter one follows!

(The stories are standalone and can be read in any order.)

LOVELY OBLIVION: JADE EXCERPT

Chapter 1

Jade

"Watch out!" One of the roadies shouted and shoved Jade, causing her to fall. She landed hard several feet away, bouncing her hip off the wooden stage.

A masculine cry of pain and a metallic crash rang through the venue when a piece from the stage lighting rig hit the roadie first then struck the theater's stage — right where Jade just stood.

Jade's heart pounded wildly, and her breathing sped up as adrenaline pumped through her body.

The roadie who shoved her, a young man with brown hair, groaned from where he lay on the floor.

Jade pushed herself up and staggered over to him, where she fell to her knees beside him.

"Are you okay?"

"I think my shoulder's dislocated," he gritted between clenched teeth.

"Okay. Stay still. I'll call for help."

She pulled her phone out of her pocket and dialed 911, her voice breathy as she rattled off the venue information and asked them to hurry.

When she hung up, she shoved her phone in her pocket and tucked a hand beneath his head, offering a small cushion against the hard stage.

He grimaced and clutched his shoulder.

"Shhhh, shhhh. Don't move. Help will be here soon," she said.

"Thank you for saving me."

The young roadie's eyes met hers, and he nodded.

One of her band's security guards, Max, ran onto the stage first. He used his earpiece radio to call for backup. He knelt by them, pulled off his SECURITY overshirt, and tucked it under the roadie's head. Jade removed her hand and sat back out of the way.

"What hurts?" he asked.

"Shoulder," the roadie grunted.

Max carefully ran his fingers over the man's shoulder and felt on it, making him hiss. She heard chatter over Max's headset but couldn't make out the words.

Max said, "It may be dislocated, but I don't think anything's broken. Try not to move. The medics are in the lobby. Two minute ETA." He turned to Jade. "You okay?"

Her hip throbbed from the impact and would probably bruise, but she didn't think her injury was serious. Her heartbeat began returning to normal.

She nodded. "Yeah, I'm okay."

Max looked at the broken rig on the stage. "What a crazy accident," he said. "I've never seen anything like this, and I've been working band security for fifteen years."

"I wonder what happened."

"Not sure." He shook his head.

Soon, the EMTs arrived and checked the roadie over. They helped him onto a stretcher and headed for the hospital.

The rest of the band and a few spectators gathered around the stage to see what happened.

Jade pulled her phone out of her pocket when the EMTs left. When she unlocked the screen, she noticed a new text message from an unknown number. *"If I can't have you, no one can. You made a mistake fucking the pretty boy fan last night. That light may have missed you this time, but you'll get your punishment soon. ~~No longer your BiggesT fan."*

Goosebumps broke out on Jade's skin. She looked around to see if she could locate the sender but no one looked suspicious. The lighting rig's fall wasn't an accident. And the culprit was nearby if he'd watched his attack fail.

* * *

Fifteen Minutes Later

"We need more security," Lyra, Jade's bandmate and best friend, insisted. She pulled her auburn hair into a ponytail and sank onto a dressing room couch.

After the attack earlier, the five members of Jade's band, Lovely Oblivion, met in the venue's dressing room.

"That's unnecessary," Jade said. They already had three security guards who toured with them and helped with venue safety. Two of them currently stood outside guarding the dressing room door, while the third, Max, filed a police report about the incident.

Lyra scoffed. "It is necessary. Someone just tried to kill you!"

Jade ran a hand through her rainbow-streaked hair with frustration. "I think it was just a scare-tactic."

"Either way, someone got hurt from it. That could have been you," Lyra said. "The attacker said you'll get your punishment soon. We need a specialized security team to catch this guy. He went 180 from adoring-fan to attacking-stalker in no-time. Who knows what he'll do next?"

"Lyra's right. We need to hire bodyguards, at least until this gets sorted out," Bex, their wiry lead singer and sometimes-fiddle-player, said. Her pixie-cut brown hair was already spiked into a Mohawk for their rock show later. "I love our guys. Max, Jake and Tyler have been with us from the start. But they're general road security and aren't trained for this shit. Stalkers and murder attempts are above their pay-grade. Let's ask the record label to hire private security for us."

Bex was typically the "voice of reason" for the band, so if she thought private security was necessary then maybe Lyra was right.

Jade sighed. "I hope we don't have to cancel tonight's performance."

She wished she knew the stalker's identity so they could nip the drama. Whoever her stalker was had followed her for years as a fan. The attack that morning pushed their status from "fan" to "stalker."

Jade was never shy or conservative — she loved to have fun. Her friends said she had "no filter" because she often said whatever popped into her head. Some people considered her rough or rude because of that, but her friends and her family loved her directness.

That fun carried over to her relationships, as well. Jade's "relationships" were a long list of one-night-stands. So far, no one made her want to commit.

Jade's reputation preceded her and everyone, including fans, knew how non-committal she could be. She assumed her stalker knew that, too. But last night's loud one-night-stand backstage with a "talented" fan that Jade mentally cataloged as "Twisty-Tongue" seemed to push the stalker over the edge.

Had her stalker tried to kill her? Or scare her? What was his goal?

"We need to call Paige," Lyra said, breaking Jade's train of thought. Paige was their manager. "Does everyone agree?"

"Yes," Bex said.

Polly, their bassist, nodded. She had styled her long blond hair in space buns — where the bottom is long and free but there are two buns on top. "Yep, sure do."

Maggie, their quiet keyboardist, also nodded. Her long black hair streamed over her shoulders.

"Fine," Jade said.

Lyra pulled out her phone and called Paige, who told them to stay put and that she would call back with an update.

It turned out, their record label didn't take the threat lightly, and assigned the band a specialized private security team.

Paige instructed them to wait in the dressing room until their new security arrived — and broke the news that the label may cancel that night's show.

* * *

Four hours later

Personal bodyguards.

Jade sighed and tapped her drum sticks on her chair restlessly. She still thought the extra security was unnecessary.

The lighting rig that clipped the roadie earlier resulted in a hospital trip and a sling but luckily no permanent damage.

The band waited in the dressing room to meet their new security and get the final word about the show. Everyone except Jade still had cell phone access and sat content in their own worlds. Security took Jade's phone and currently kept the band detained in the dressing room.

Jade glared at Lyra from across the room. Calling their manager had been all Lyra's idea.

Lyra must have felt the evil-eye because she looked up from her phone and flipped Jade off in response.

"I'm reconsidering your 'best friend' title," Jade said.

Lyra laughed. "You'll thank me for this later. I promise," she said.

"Highly doubtful."

Lyra and Jade were friends long before they became bandmates. They'd become quick friends in elementary school and stuck together since.

They formed their punk rock band Lovely Oblivion with Polly, Bex, and Maggie, three other musicians they'd met during college. They hit it big and signed a record deal in their early 20s.

Jade loved it and wouldn't have changed a thing.

Well, except this stalker thing. If she'd known the fan's actions would escalate like this, she would have nipped it sooner. Now, it impacted other fans.

The third date of the new tour. A sold-out rock show. Out of everything that happened, the potential cancellation probably pissed Jade off the most. She hated disappointing the fans. Thousands of people rearranged their schedules, spent money, and made plans to see their performance, but one selfish jerk might ruin everyone's night.

Jade growled loudly right as the door opened.

Blue eyes met hers, first with surprise, then with what she guessed might be amusement, at her outburst.

Their owner — a tall, toned hunk with dark hair — strolled into the room behind Tawny, the band's tiny female tour manager. Four other built guys followed them. Tawny looked even smaller than normal standing beside them, even wearing her favorite high-heeled boots. These guys practically screamed "badass military" with their chiseled bodies, tattoos, and overall demeanor.

As Tawny closed the door tightly behind them, Jade glimpsed their normal security guard, Tyler, standing watch in the hallway.

"Hey, ladies," Tawny said. She moved further into the room.

Tawny looked meek to those who didn't know her, but she was really a force to be reckoned with — her job required backbone and grit. As their road manager, she coordinated all their stops, hotels, crews, and venues. She made everything run smoothly while the band was on the road.

Their actual manager, Paige, ran the image, tour schedule, and financial side of things; Tawny made the tour happen efficiently.

"Meet your new security team," Tawny said.

She pointed to Mr. Blue Eyes.

His dark hair was longer on top and shorter on the sides. No wedding ring. A tattoo peeked out from the neck of his blue dress shirt. Though he wore dressy clothes currently, he had a predatory look about him that signaled he wouldn't hesitate to fight at a moment's notice. The gun on his hip amplified the intimidating image.

Jade's interest piqued immediately. This guy had an interesting story to tell, and she wanted to hear it all.

Tawny continued, "This is Ryker Vittroli. He's your new head of security. Whatever he says goes. No fighting him, ladies."

The words were out of Jade's mouth before she could stop them, "Oh Tawny, I plan to fight with him — All. Night. Long."

Ryker's eyes flicked to Jade. He said, "I'm going to have my hands full with you, aren't I?"

"I sure hope so," Jade said with a grin. "You can fill your hands with me anytime."

Ryker held her gaze but cleared his throat. There was definitely amusement in his eyes, and she thought she almost sensed a smile under the stoic surface.

Tawny scowled. "Jade, behave. There will be no harassment on my tour," she warned. "Ladies, I expect you to give Mr. Vittroli your full cooperation. His team is here for your safety, not your pleasure. Consider them off-limits unless it's safety-related."

Tawny settled on a nearby chair, an irritated look on her face, and she gestured for Ryker to start.

Ryker's voice rumbled, "Good afternoon. I'm the director of Vittroli Security Specialists — VSS for short. We are a private team of former Navy SEALs who specialize in security for high-profile clients. Your record label hired us to protect you all until Jade's stalker situation resolves. We stay until we catch the stalker."

He rapped his knuckles against the table. "I understand you're used to a relaxed security regime, so I need you to pay attention."

"Don't dodge us. We can't protect you if you disappear on us. We will take you wherever you want to go so you can do whatever you want to do — as long as it's safe. We're on your side. We want to keep your lives as normal as possible. But we have to keep in mind that stalkers are persistent, crazy, and could go after any of you to hurt Jade. So there will be some necessary changes to your routine. Especially yours, Jade."

Though the time was probably inappropriate, Jade loved the sound of Ryker's deep voice rumbling her name.

He continued, "Any special requests or issues run past me. Go nowhere alone. You are more vulnerable by yourself. Backstage bathroom? Hotel suite? We check first. Every time. Walking from the bus or limo to the hotel or the venue? Never alone. Understood?"

Mumbled assent came from around the room.

Ryker pointed to each of the men in line beside him. First to the tall man next to him, whose long brown hair was pulled back into a ponytail. "This is Drake." Then to the man next to Drake with a shaved head. "Benny." The third man had a buzz cut and a sharp jaw. "Roark." The fourth man had buzz cut blond hair and an eagle tattoo on his forearm. "Diesel." He gestured to all of them. "This is the VSS team. Don't trust anyone you don't see here."

He continued, "We'll be training your normal security to prevent these kinds of incidents moving forward and will also work with each venue's teams to ensure your safety. You will get to know all of us very well until we resolve this."

Jade asked, "What about tonight's show? It's sold out. We're already here. Can we still play?"

Tawny answered. "No, absolutely not. We have to reschedule this show. There's no time to safety-check everything at this venue before you go on. We've already sent out the press release. Tonight's show is canceled."

Exactly what Jade had feared. All those disappointed fans... Anger shot through her.

"Dammit!" Jade jumped to her feet and hurled her drum sticks across the room, narrowly missing Tawny. "First our roadie, and now our fans. Who does this stalker think he is? He can be pissed at me, but he can't fuck with the band. It's got to be someone on tour. Who else would know what hotels we're staying at and what my room numbers are? Who else could have watched all that go down earlier with the lighting rig? And who else could've heard me fucking Twisty-Tongue last night in the dressing room? Definitely someone on tour."

"Twisty-Tongue?" Ryker asked with a raised eyebrow.

Jade's angry gaze turned on him.

"Really? That's all you took from what I said? Un-fucking-believable, Mr. Head of Security."

Shockingly, Ryker rolled his eyes at her.

She crossed her arms over her chest. She'd thrown her sticks too soon. If she had waited a minute, she could have hurled them at him and it would have been so much more satisfying.

He said, "No, that's not all I took from your tantrum but that was the one tidbit I didn't already know." His eyes challenged hers.

He continued, "We are well aware the stalker is likely someone on tour. We've already started background checks on everyone. We checked out the phone number from the text message, but it was a prepaid burner phone with no identifying information. Until we find out more from the background checks, it's wait-and-see. Which is why we need to keep you all safe in the meantime."

His gaze flicked around the room, and he addressed everyone.

"For now, the plan is get back on the bus for the next leg of the tour. We'll arrive at the next venue early and set up for the day. The most important thing is keeping everyone safe while my team finds the attacker."

Jade wasn't sure whether to be pissed off or impressed. Ryker had serious-attitude hidden under that professional demeanor. Now, if only she didn't look forward to challenging him so much.

Get the rest of Lovely Oblivion: Jade (Book 1) on Amazon!